Towards The Path

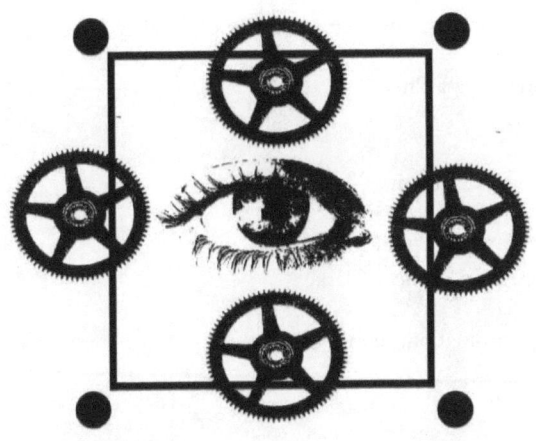

Published by endaStampa Press
Toronto, Ontario

Email: endapress@gmail.com

Book Illustrator: Patrick O'Malley Burke
Book Layout Designer: Spencer Clarke

Book Editorial Coordination: Jennie Clarke

First Edition

Canada, United Kingdom, USA

ISNB: 978-0987773982

A journey through the light

Towards The Path

A Tale by Patrick O'Malley Burke

Tales of old and new looking from a distance right back at you. Things we read grow into light then find a heart so full of might. Don't close your eyes for too long, you may miss what went wrong. The air goes dark within these days like a storming of catastrophic haze. Time stands still for no beating heart though through an opening time pulls apart, only the knowing will find its way, looking deep from our yesterday. For the yesterday tears do tell such tales, of cruelty and misfortune only found in such Mystery Tales

Chapter One

The Opening

Shivers found the abandoned walls, tormented from all hallowed screams, the decades of tortured screeching found of shadows passing through this emptied room. Quickening to the sound of demise jumps out to the scratching's from many years of abandonment. A room like this could only hold mischief, misery, of ghosts finding their victims, the innocent are not safe within these walls, though what is lurking under the floor is much worse. Loathing pressed into dead dream with no way to heal. Only the stillness will worship the wait for it's unsuspecting subject to walk towards such powers. Though within the evil, the positive   lives   not   far   behind

Walking towards an old empty room a distant figure finds a door open, part of the floor has been damaged, and it looks like someone was looking for something. While walking closer into the room light finds the face of the eyes of a man, he mutters out to the dark

"What is this"?

"It looks like someone has departed in a hurry"?

From the damaged floor a feeling that he cannot describe finds him, he looks towards an opening within the surface, finding an old wooden box covered with wax. He takes hold of the box and with his fingernails he scrapes away the wax. After a short while the box is free from the wax leaving him to look at it with more curiosity, finding a strange symbol burned into the top, it looks like two birds of some kind. Opening the box he finds a small note and on the bottom of the note embedded with wax a pin with something on the end. The note reads

"If you want to see the truth, take the pin and place it in the centre point of your hand and clap four times."

The man ponders for a short while and thinks to himself

"What the hell."

Placing the pin in his hand and with for slow hesitant clap's he finds a small pain as the pin enters his skin. Within seconds he

Falls to the ground tumbling into a deep like dream state. While now in dream he listens to a voice calling out

"Do you actually know what is inside of a working clock, have you ever wondered how they keep time or why is it that we hold time so close. What if inside the working mechanisms hidden deep within was something completely uninterested in what we know as time, living beside your dreams, listening to your last thought before you fall asleep. As you take a gasp of air recording the beat of the heart listening to everything we do, Sending everything back somewhere so very far from us into a world that feeds upon our thoughts and dreams. We the living, the breathing experiments, subjects of flesh expected and unknowingly to give a lifetime of thoughts to something unknown, under the pretence of time."

Soon you will drift into deep dream

Why do we forget some of our past and at the same time can remember only certain moments, we have to ask ourselves did that really happen?

Who is fooling you into thinking this and why. For what use can the human thinking be to others. I will show you the way things really are so you can see the truth within this world, can you imagine what your about to see, some things are so large that the mind has problems finding reasoning so it makes the best definition towards the way it wants you to find comfort. This is the way of how most people never realize what's really going on in their lives. Soon you will drift into deep dream this will keep you safe from any harm, all that will be is your conscious will find its king and make shape within dream. Some of us can decide what we will become in dream, though I must tell you that it is only the chosen that can do such a thing.

Shades of bright vibrant colours started overtaking shapes of reds into blues, tasselled with the yellows and green making the most magnificent of wisdom scopes translating to all. While all this was happening within the centre frame started forming character into shape. More colours found the manifestation, reproduction of the man's new form. After a while a voice called out.

"Open"

"Open friend"

"Awaken and open friend it is time to see what is known as the real world, do not worry you cannot be harmed and for reasons to us we shall call you REAN. You must remember this, for now only this so open and see for the first time".

REAN opened his eyes.

"What? Is this he gasped, why have I been brought hear"?

His other world was now truly abandoned and the arrival into abstraction has been completed. Worlds of time world of few falling into the long forgotten new, this will be found, towards within oneness a journey for the lost now found, correcting the mind from old to new, find what is really true.

Some words from the past have been blocked only time will see what can be, truth from dream they say was unseen though through lost abandonment true our new ambitions will find the true.

REAN steps back calling out to himself

"What is this? Am I awake or dreaming? Someone please help me I want to wake up I don't feel to good"

Staggering back his eyes struggle to stay open, his legs start to buckle beneath him. A blow to the ground, with a crash the ground gives way, REAN shouts out

"Help me!"

Now falling towards the ending towards the maze of the forgotten inner world, a world that grows within sincerity, the living is not walking though feeling is the becoming towards an appropriate new living form, without air to function, no need for air when this physique has long since abandoned the physical and become physic, physical the embayment that keeps with to send out. No need for bodily words, no, this actuality communicates with the use of thought, they use the quietness to grow and become more in tune with each other. This stops and reason to maltreatment, no jealousy can be found in this frame, only space within, to find reasoning then to move on to the next fragment of this inner worldly living universe, within dream are so many places to visit, some call this habitation the maze of contemplations, the holding of the old into new finding everything that can't fail to recall. Total embodiment recall.

Towers of holdings Column high, standing deep within, mountains in mass, standing above below and all-around deeper and profounder never ending, the holding of the emending. Taking into a world of extreme following the surreal towards everything new a new life comes without vengeance calling though through a new way of living and seeing from many thoughts that come together as one, they become like an mathematical remedy becoming physical complete volume to then shower and hold within truth that becomes supplementary within the all abandonment striving to complete success, Evolving towards unaffectedness healing and increasing positivity in a new world hidden from within.

Deep tunnels from the dark desires from all human minds becoming togetherness with a new reforming life calling out to the helplessness crying out from this falling human depth soon all we be apparent and become an understanding within how and what is expected within this new dimension of the thinking within living minds, the new born within. They stand with you and for the wanting, the very disgusting addictions the human body has to endure every living second of the beating heart, no, this way of life is affected from nothing like that. Soon this would be, living in verse so wonderful this feeling that becoming from everything new, standing without disaster in mind finding the way that has been only made from wishing and dreaming. This demand from the mind can at first be overwhelming to cause strange visionary overlaps that can create the opal contradiction.

This is overcome with deep thinking towards calmness almost in meditations sounds of the abandonment, though with contemplation this can be in a controlled averment, taking hold of the sinister and reforming into overwhelming objective and direct objectives that once found shall never be forgotten holding within and moulding a new quantity that is how we see and achieve everything new leaving behind our old ways, they just become without purpose, collapsing in the negative broken world while all new thinking holds true. A way of sighted without seeing, sounds strange and can be difficult though through particle holds true.

Holding on to everything he knew, REAN wanted so much to open his eyes though actuality fighting his reality was becoming something very different than what he had been used to, a witness of the ever changing feelings and thoughts, what is this ascending sensation? Reanimation of all atmospheres creating energy all new, Landing at last, with a smash though without any kind of discomfort, everything is too much to handle, and a state of unconsciousness was needed to save his first time experience of the inner world.

"You"

"You wake now", reached out a distant voice

Finding his feet REAN dared to open his eyes, standing in front of him, gazing into his eyes was Hassam the living embodiment of life itself, towards the meandering heart beating seeker lived all new. Hassam lifted his arms towards Rean calling out, "welcome, o welcome, it has been said for many years that you would reach us and now hear you are, it is like a living tale, we have some much to show you."

Flying past their heads finds body metamorphic symbolic physique twisting out within, the opened opal like sky, filled with its own living screams, the only way to be described was a thousand dreams within a carrier imagined frame. Disorder of any from any purposes was only to play with Rean's already penetrating concentration.

"You see this is not your world anymore, No, this is our world within every mind we live and find you, playing with what purpose we feel fitting", calling out Hassam in a menacing way.

"I don't understand why you have chosen me? Why? Why me? And what the hell is this place?" cried out Rean

He just kept repeating himself over and over again "why me? I just don't understand?"

He was so tired, and to find answers was something so very far from him, abandoned and confused in a strange new world, everything felt so confusing. "Am I awake or dreaming? I just can't understand what is happening to me" he felt like he was about to fall unconscious, "is this, what happens to people who run to dead dream's?" He remembers back to when he was a small boy excepting the world to fall to his feet and take it all without thinking of anyone but himself. Shifting his head to a side "I just wanted to be free, I didn't realize what I was doing to my life, it is so long ago it could have been not me and some other person, time has gone so fast, I really don't want to look back anymore and look to what will be."

In a less menacing way Hassam replied "we cannot help our past, though now we can make better things, if we look at what can be then the forward thinking will always win, to think back, can be constructive   for   the   mind,   helps   things   grow.

Within the awareness forming a new reality that finds us and Hassam asked if he could show Rean the words from writings he used when first entering this inner world, as he found them very useful and wanted to pass them on, think it would help.

"Yes please, do" replied Rean

Towards the opening found new light a transcending feeling that should stay, maybe for a while anyway, without distant treasures it could not be, finding distance between what will stand and what will be in hand, crazy to think of so many scary thoughts all locked up and angry and dissatisfied with everything. The twisting and turning of mood spin old and new could find anything to do with you, then all to the tick, tick, from life's second clock you find a reason within the stay that at last make you want to visit and stops you running away, what now for the negative creep, putting all that far, far away. This all new feeling, why, its, so new what has come over you? It's so wonderful to open your eyes, seeing life is such a wonderful surprise, so now to the bright ended lights dancing around you, it's not so bad with this positive shower coming your way, yes, o yes, how wonderful, can this really be true? Is this the end of negative creep wanting everything for nothing, o so unique? Makes us stronger"

Look at the way its shadow has gone falling from every day nothing that would overcome. Beside yourself at last, and listening to every word, inside this new sound your hearing life sing. So beautiful is the sound of everything around the new you, past the old from into new, remembering everything you need too, towards this fresh thinking new finding arise like the sunrise of the new second from morning sunlight end day.

Soon this will find you, play this song every day, never to be forgotten and shall be sent out to others around you. Yes, at first things will become difficult towards the mind, though through time contentment will overcome the old and provide you with your all new, showering you with confidence, standing you solid fighting all that may go to the wrong, beside this fight how you will be strong, beside friend or for what will be is how you flow, between two destructive lines, light is what you'll find, hiding ready when you need it the most ready and willing to be the host, listening in to all that is to be said, ready to back you up with a ship shape of the ticking from times misleading clocks.

Never forget these words you hear for the works from times gear are the upmost truth, that will be said and pilot you strait towards your positive gate. For this shall be sold from tales of new and taken from old, listen to the silence, within its silvery might truth is dancing destroying all negative nasty's so full of spite.

Most of the time we see what we want too without thinking how that can affect the people around you, every action has a reaction to others , new and old, like a stone falling into the sea, finding its way beside one, two, then three. What if the stone found its way on the back of a swan, finding its way just the same though without causing any kind of woe, promising the swan that nothing would go wrong? Seeking the truth is hard to do without the light to find its way make new from old, stones to gold.

So if you can remember what has been told may be from somewhere new it will find you, for this has been waiting for so long and now you have found me , just like an old friend, plenty of love between these words and very useful all the same, nothing to confuse you.

So step back and trust what will be, find your reasoning and work on what you will, for this will grow you strong and soon becoming the new will be a part of your thinking, it won't be so hard to find yourself anymore, coming forward within the light towards the ever changing truth living inside you. Amending the forgotten your ways that twist in your dreams and tie you up, in storming's all a shadowy mess pulling at every little disorder in that head, little poor you won't need that blue, inset towards the light is heading your way remember the words to shed a tear.

This reasoning is far from what you want to know though it will be of use to you in many ways; if you can remember the good within your thinking then in many ways you can hold the key to open many new doors of perception, your awareness of one's self

Discovery and knowing will lead you towards many new doorways within the mind and through the living world. To know the right and the giving will enable your new sense of awareness, growing within a forward blossom within your soul. Listen to everything around you, the sounds that we tend to forget or just pass by, if you can attend to what is around you this will also allow you to find the within all about you. At the moment your world is hiding from you, yes, it is there though you cannot listen because your doorways are closed, though ready for you to open, just waiting for your senses to unlock so you can start the becoming. Your given eyes to see though do you really see what is around you,

For what is around you tends to hide from the one that open his mind and see the real world to his full. To start this new journey of self-awareness forget everything from what we call your past, this is because everything you think you know has polluted your mind in thinking that this is the way of life, when really it was put within your head to do the opposite, shall we not see if we have been blindfolded, can we not see, if we have no words, shall we not hear the truth if told nothing but lies.

Words are put into your head so that you think that they are the true verses of life, a word can be a wonderful romance and useful thing, though in the same sense this can cut into your spine leaving you helpless believing the untruth extinguishing your intelligences and eating away at certainty, this inevitability of brain washing leading you into misadventure and deluding what could have been a wonderful start into the real inner world.

14

When you start to see your true self meaning, o you hold such phenomenon of meaningful living this makes everything so new to your wisdoms, explanation will become the new way of listening to everything here and now.

Can we want for nothing and live a contented life, for within the sky do you see the bird flying free, and for what do you see? Just one living from blissful and content, Should we not listen and absorb for what is around us. And to abandon this want for everything and actual fix, the sickening can no longer go on, no, a amending shall abscond this putrefaction of the awareness and we shall show you the new way within the inner world.

Falling towards tomorrow is everything that would have been without a seconds thought, the breath from all beautiful new showering thoughtfulness, caressing new life from stillness to a dance from sky fall new form and in you, tomorrow's war has terminated, forward thinking is the new approach towards this ever lightened vision within you, towards a journey so new only the everything holding this fullness of knowledge will hold you forever, giving you the sight within to become all new and find a way, that is your way into everything you wanted too, though could not imagine how to find it.

Lay down your anger, walk towards me, we shall not take from you, no, only we shall give, and show you all that is true. So come and stand beside me, we shall, you will, live and listen towards everything since abandoned thoughts long lost though through your shadows shall crawl the new, find what will be.

This towering surrendering has nothing but the love for you, as I stand and listen within you all I hear is the scream from your nothing world, past true past old, right through you is where they find your uncertainty, how they play within that playground. Following the right direction will enable your gates closed to any such thing, and hold strong away to anything so wrong.

O... beautiful effervescent confrère let him in, for this light echoes within all, do not close this door, hold me within you, I shall not wound your friendship of such knowledge. Hold this day within, towards ever changing light that finds this dance. This day ever so beautiful with your essences next to me, shall it not die, no, this still to the ever changing second of the breath from our sun lighted day, let it show you the way.

Pick up your ever changing day and walk to me, we have so much to see, so very much is within you and all you have to do is repair what has been, o dear friend I fall to your feet and become a part of everything that we will show you, tranquillity finds the ever changing day without yesterday's alterations, becoming unclear to the sight from shaded judgments, that shadowed unwanted child, still to the night waiting for the sign that everything is all right.

Still from the night that finds all your fright though finding a new, this will hold true. Becoming everything you wanted it too, towards the inner finding your hunger wisdom child, crying out for more, more, more, what you will do without this horrid

Nothing inside you? Screaming out for everything you don't want to be, though through the inside out faced child, telling everyone inside a spiteful tale. Though listening to what is told to you then to find reason showing the negative creep the doorway within the never-ending fall, making the darkness ever so small, shallow to the quickening of darkness tale.

Do you remember when all was so new? When you thought you could do anything? Anything and everything was in your reach. Well, it was, it was just the wrong path that found you. Let it be known on this day, from this second your new path is opened and towards the fantastic. Written from your past you see nothing, holding on to something so strong is very difficult, the definition from truth within you're never ending simulating life line. This has been untruthful, though now we can take you away from this confusion and help you gain great knowledge through the power of positive thinking and self-awareness.

"Interesting words, though I don't understand what they call from me?" Rean say stepping backwards

"Soon you will, and all will come clearer, the words will grow within your mind and become a part of you, finding the real inside your mind, finding your humanity, soon you will feel so very different than how you are today, we have been observing you for a long time, and not just you."

For years now hidden within the workings of the timepieces planted listening and observing mechanisms, recording from

Many years ago. We have been watching and listening to all of what you call life, yes, life times of living have been recorded and studied closely, so that we could find someone that we think could help us find the way into our middle world. And we found you.

Me?

Yes, we wanted someone who was lost, between both worlds, without knowing, we knew you would be the one, and for a long time-now

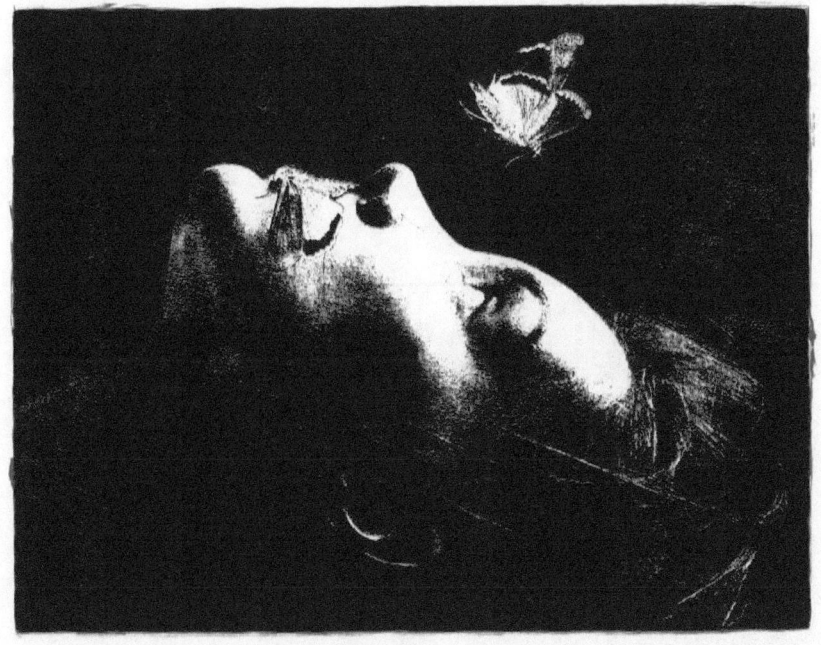

Between both worlds

Chapter Two

Within the shadows

Within the shadows from new and old dances ghosts from distance untold, screams from hollows past lives hatred burned in deep, the true abandonment that finds the new that follows within this world, if we cannot live within this world, then we shall come and take you, own your last word we shall, forget your memory bliss, no that you will fall and miss. The area became dark, the shifters began to appear surrounding Rean, breathing became very difficult; he started to breakout in a red painful rash. "What is this? I don't understand? Oh, what is going on?" he screamed out.

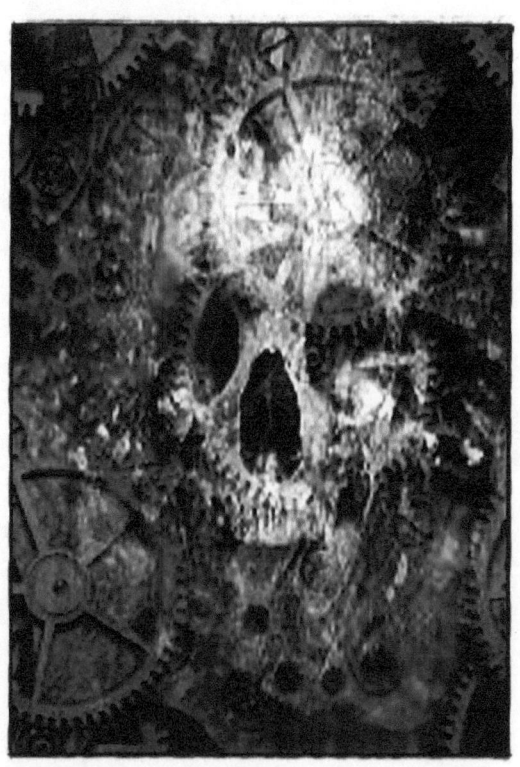

Shivers found him fast, "what is this lack of self-worth? How can things change so quickly?" he cried out

Then he remembered what was read out to him by the guide Hassam, deep within his mind he reasoned with his feelings, "I am in control, I am, I am in control, I must find my inner strength" he lost conscious for a while.

He came too wondering if he was awake or dreaming, like shifts of light, ever changing to the second to the mood bending. Rean's image began to change, flickering like a light going on and off, his image was changing fast, as fast as a heartbeat from the ever quickening of light found Rean changing from his past presence to his future presence, like a visual image of recorded time from past and forthcoming. One second he's a small child the next he's middle age, and then he's an old man repeating over and over. No man could take much more of this, what was this? This vision of many years passing within seconds, how could it be?

This abandoned thinking, from distance and a long way from his many years of living in his old world, where most things found reason, without thinking he would find reason, living day after day, the very reason of his life was shaded by day to day living. Like many of his kind Rean had fallen into the trap of everyday living and become to accustomed to this way of so called life. Though now it was to be a very different way of thinking, of living. While he was flickering in and out of all the years of his life so far, memories found him, a struggle for survival within his head, and now the realization of what was happening. "I

Remember so many things, so many things" he repeated over and over, "I never knew I had achieved so much in my life"

A voice found him

"Awaken friend"

"Awaken"

Rean's eyes opened, standing above him was two long white ghostly figures, hovering above his face. He looked deep within their forms, hovering over him, looking at his new surroundings, a new world of many new and extraordinary moving existing presences. "What, where am I, a few minutes ago I was talking to someone called Hassam? Who was that? Was I dreaming?"

"You will encounter many new and exciting new living life presences, do not worry, for this is the way you will find what and who you are, for in your world many things blocked you from the real way of thinking and this was not so good for you, we are trying not to send you into your own self, seeing so many new things at once, this can become harmful at first, so please go slow with your thinking." One of the strange new floating figures spoke in a gentle and calming way. Their eyes looked deep within Rean's eyes, like they were caressing his mind within the kind words.

This way of living could only be for one thing, to manipulate.

Rean found himself standing towards to figures, they spoke, "follow us, come and we will show you where it is safe for you,

23

come now, quickly friend, quickly we cannot waste any more time"

With haste they set away towards empty looking deep long hallways prepared of many strange doorways. "What could this be and why have I been taken hear, why or why?" Rean could not help himself from panicking. Falling towards an opening they fell deep within the darkened doorway.

Falling deep within the darkness, surrounded by faces coming in and out of the darkness, words echoing around, crying out "surrender, surrender to the nothing it's so easy" faces of anguish, tormented by their own mind lifecycle that went so wrong, they just keep on coming, with no let up the most terrifying ghostly faces sending shivers down Rean's spine.

When will this end? He wondered, and then all went completely dark, a cracked lost face finds the last moment of light and comes forward towards Rean calling out to him " do you want something?" the most terrifying feelings found Rean sending him into a shiver while trying to get his words out. "Can you tell me how to get out of here?" stuttered Rean

"Why did you come here? You're not allowed in here, get out, get out or we will keep your face and send you on your way!" shouted the pale white face

"Please… I just want to get out of here, please, I don't want to bother you anymore, just tell me how to get out?" Stammered Rean "all you have to do is look deep within yourself, for that is everything and what is everything is just you, so all you have to do is find the real inside you, find what is real and you will have the key, trust me" the hovering face kindly replied and swiftly disappeared.

Rean started to think, he closed his eyes and tried to remember the words called out to him a while back, "it's all within me, all within me" thinking deep and just using his mind to see, Rean could visualise a light in front of him, it had a warm yellowed glow, walking slowly, cautiously holding out his arms waling deeper into the light, first his legs then all of himself.

With a safer sensation flowing through his body he felt like something exciting and new had just experienced his awareness. "How did I do that? That was amazing, I did it, I believed in myself for the first time and it all paid off, so it is true I hold the key.

Without knowing how he found his way out of such dark foreboding dwelling hidden within a timeless expanse, not many can survive such a hole.

This light is still with him ascending from the outer world that says that someone from the outer world is thinking of him.

Chapter Three

Dead Tree's

Rean found himself standing in a new space, this time he was outside on a faraway dream scape controlled by dreams and nightmares, he would have to keep his wits about him this time. He was standing in front of a tree, though this tree looked a little bit different than what he has come to know as a tree, as this wooden giant was moving, and moaning, he walked forward and noticed the trees structure was made from human body's, churning and swirling around screeching out a haunting sound, shivers found Rean's spine, the smell made him wrench.

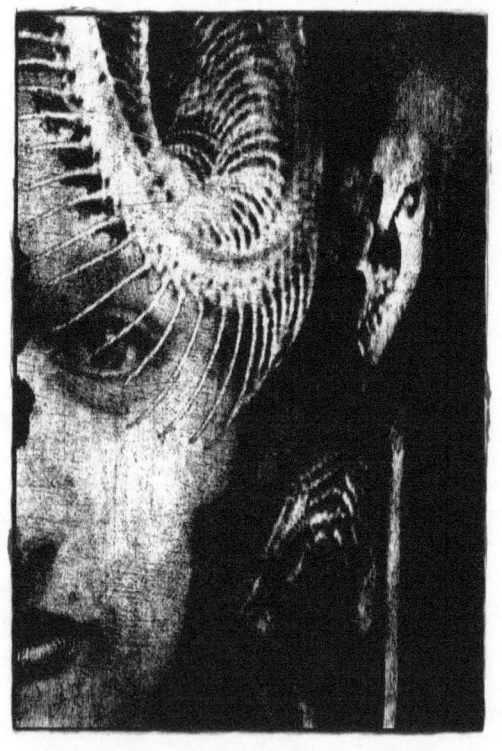

Shivers

"What is this?" he screamed

Rean looked upwards and as far as he could see the forest of human trees was in front of him, the sound was horrific, its wasn't human voices that found him, no, even though the trees looked like there where made from humans the sound was like something he had never listened to before, a sound truly horrific. The only way was forward, he was about to set on his way when Rean noticed a small figure approaching him. What could it be? Rean shouted out "hey there...hello can you help me? Where am I? Can you help me?"

The being became closer, "don't touch the trees! Whatever you do don't touch the trees, if you touch the trees they will take your body and you will become a walking ghost, please sir step away from the trees" the approaching being shouted while shaking his fist.

Rean stepped away from the trees with haste, "thank you, thank you for saving my life, please forgive me though who are you? What is your name my friend?"

"Yes, I like the word friend, and my name is Aldus, I am your guide for a short while, and will lead you to your next part of this journey"

Aldus was from the UConn tribe, a tribe of helpers made from the goodness within all dreams; they only appear when needed, and always come true. His appearance was like looking at a kind old man, with a bent over back, along black coat and white flowing hair, his eyes was to be said to give a settling feeling when looked into a very kind old man.

"My name is Rean, and again I thank you for saving me"

"I already know your name, and I know most of what you are, don't you worry yourself Rean, I am here for you and to help you find what you're looking for, we have to go through the forest of human trees, take this my friend it will protect you from the trees"

Aldus held out his hand and presented a red orb to Rean.

"Take this, it will help you through where we have to go next, come, place it above your head"

Rean reach forward and grabbed the red orb and held it towards his head, the orb recognized Rean and began to glow an amazing red haze and covered Rean with a protected afterglow.

"Thank you Aldus!"

"That's it, now you're safe; though try not to touch anything while we walk through the forests, there's all sorts of mischiefs hidden within the forests"

They set of through the twisting tormented trees of human flesh; the orb was protecting Rean from the horrific noises.

"This way my friend, this way" pointed Aldus towards an opening in the woods.

They set off walking through, the deeper they get the darker it became. The moving twisting moaning groaning giants overhead all-around, look at you everywhere you look, someone is looking back at you with nothing inside their eye's, tormented screaming of true abandonment is storming everywhere, sometimes you can see the walking ghosts, lost nothing and nowhere to go.

The greyness plays with your mind, faces appear then disappear, was that really their or was that your mind, did you hear that? What was that screaming, was it the call for your name. Don't forget not to touch the tree's going through one's mind, this never ending twisting and turning, swirling in the lurking the darkest of dark, hiding within everything that wants to control your thinking, this uneasiness makes you feel so very uncomfortable, oh what will become of you? Remember don't touch the trees. Listen to the crying of uncertainty towards the greyed eyed monsters faltering and seeing you everywhere you walk, try not to make so much noise think on all the darkness, it's becoming so loud, shush and don't touch the tree's.

Falling around you roots everywhere you walk looking like arms coming to get you, caressing your thoughts the way you don't want them to. Keep walking, keep walking, don't look away for too long and keep your face up and remember don't touch the trees.

They want you so bad, an addiction of blood is what they want, your body is there food it makes them ever so strong, the towering steaming grounds filled with a nightmare sound, do run, now walk through with a quick step to the flinch of a heart beating fighting lurking sight. Weaving around every tree are body's swirling calling out, help me, save me, just a touch, help us, don't leave us all we want is your touch. Keep walking and pick up that pace, keep walking try not to leave a trace. Remember don't touch the trees, step to step looking forward now, listening to the howling the screaming cry's fill this darkened space, misery is everywhere so you must stay true, stay within the you, the one you know and trust that's always good to you. That's the one who will get you through.

This darkened hazed way was becoming more difficult to walk through, the trees where becoming more intense with their screaming and winding, every stride was becoming so exhausting, more and more the twisting weaving roots wear becoming stronger, all over this soil lived strange looking insects, maggots of new kind eating away at everything in sight, this was truly the darkest gloomiest part of his journey so far.

Dark of night hold me tight, don't let the trees take my body I don't want to walk with the ghosts, for the fright of this darkened wood smells of rotting flesh dripping with their

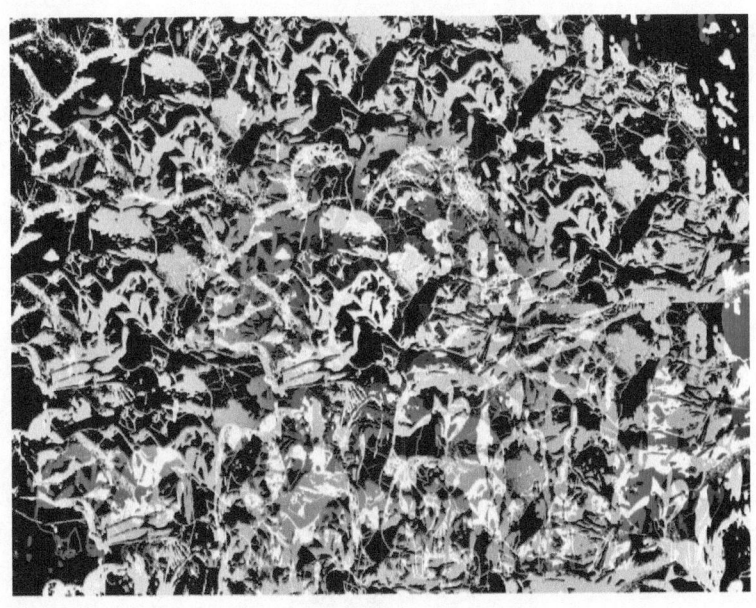

Blood, the human forgotten was dancing on this night only to the sound of shivering unforgiving fright. Blood dripping into the

roots twisting and meandering around human body flesh, arms holding out for salvation, saving the dead would not be for the wise, only an idiot would attempt such a thing. Slow to the sound of crying nothings walking a maze of twisting flesh, this stench of the rotting way, showing Rean how to escape from this moving hell. And now for the way to carry him through, for what will become of him when he reaches the end, the opening was not that far away, the smell was over whelming to the point of falling over with the lack of clean air. Oh darkness please stop and let him see the lightened ending way, the seeker way walking through this living hell, the walk of the dead should never be seen, hold on, nearly there and remember don't touch the trees. They hunger for your flesh, growing so high toward the darkened sky, why or why, do the corpses cry so and for what evil made such a dwelling of tortured sadness, will it all ever end?

Towards the creeping lives nothing but death, lying and deceitful the living trees for their flesh, leaving their tortured ghosts to walk confused and in a forgotten mess.

When would the ending arrive? How long will it be before this endless walking, excruciating and mind stretching, towards a large tree they walked, with an opening in the centre of the tree, it looked like a giant mouth ready to swallow them both, so dark and foreboding, what is this? And why are they going towards such a frightening expanse.

Walking closer and closer Rean was starting to feel that something was going to happen to him, they finally reach the opening of the large old tree, and Rean asked "so do we go into the darkness?"

Chapter Four

Into the light

Aldus looked at Rean and held out his arm and in his hand was glowing eyes, with an amazing blue glow reaching the outline of Rean's face. "So Rean... now it is time for you to see" said Aldus

Rean hunched back his shoulders scratched his head and said "To see, to see what?"

"Now, looking into the eye Rean, look deep into the eye and see, and see"

The eye started to cast out shifts of lights, finding their way into the trees opening, lightening up the darkened hole at the entrance of large old tree.   "Now look Rean" called out Aldus. The light found the dark and opened up the light within, how beautiful became this ever glance, that second became so new from all the darkness and intimidating frightfulness became a wonderful feeling of sincerity, oh this new light found the goodness within all this darkened sickness, oh how wonderful. This was the new light, the new day within the inside out way, all was to be forgotten and to find love within a new light, for this light was the new way of seeing through all the saddened screams.

Aldus called out "come now Rean, we have to travel through the tree, don't be fooled into thinking where going into an old tree, trust me when I say this, come now… it is time, follow me, and follow me, Rean."

"what can I say Aldus, for the light I see in front of me is so beautiful and I cannot but help myself, I ponder, though know that this is what should be, like the first opening of my eyes in the morning after a good night's sleep, oh Aldus this feels so right, yes I will follow you, and give you my trusting heart."

They walked into the light and followed the channels mazing into the brightened magnificence, a towering of new energies, finding every beating breath of the pounding heart, oh for this new light that finds them, showing the way into everything, like the new born babies eyes so full of life. This light, this beautiful never ending light, shall find their way into the something so new. Rean could see rows of lights forming different pathways, and bulling walls on wall.

It soon became apparent that there was only one path to take. And this one they would gladly follow. After seeing all that misery and suffering feeling this new animated way, one could only trust such a feeling and a passage way. This freshness, oh... this ever essence of life within his heart was so wonderful, tear of joy found his eyes that allowed him to follow his way through the lighted shine, beaming all around him. They followed towards the path and carried on through the light.

Aldus said "you may touch the lighted wall if so desire, see what happens."

Rean touched the wall, as soon as Rean's hand touched the wall he felt amazing warmth within his heart, it was like feeling total love, he was helpless to the love inside his heart, his body surrendering everything to the feelings that had overtaken him. This light that had surrounded, the wonderful everything around and beyond this living sole amending any impurities that had followed from the dead tree forest, following the new light within Rean could see things in a new light, reasoning with things that normally appeared unapproachable and now he could walk through anything.

"Rean, come now... we have to carry on" shouted Aldus

Rean dragged his hand from the wall and started to follow Aldus "ok I'm coming Aldus, that was an amazing feeling"

"That was the goodness within the light what you was feeling, soon you will have that with you and be able to control your abandonments nothing ghosts" replied Aldus

They carried on into the light, shifts of colours would pass them by, with a sensory ease.

Follow the light find the strait within all that is new, we shall love you within, shout out to the light I love this life... I love this life, cast away any negative slay, from today everything will become ever clear new, let it be known from this day all the goodness will find your kingdom, this ever clear realm shall kiss you, hold you, be everything within this inner earth child, surrendering yourself to all and that is what will be , for it is not the dark within you that will overcome your mind, no... it is known that on this day the light will find you, look after you, hold your every wish and open the doors towards this new day of thinking, the abandonment shall rule the darkened hallows and find your strength, so that within and for ever you shall hold this within you, a new friend is waiting for your willingness to walk through the doors of light.

Shout I am, I will be... and this is

For within your own temple stands your monument, look forward and stand in front of that doorway, and let it be known to all your hear standing your own with the love of everything inside of your heart, ready to belong within the living kingdom, No   longer   a   living   ghost   walking.

Feel the air around you, touch everything as you where new born, for this day is the new start within your new day. Hold on to this and follow me towards everything new that shall hold you strong for what will be, this is just the start for you, inhale in that beautiful air, and for every gasp... it is a new brick towards your new temple of strength.

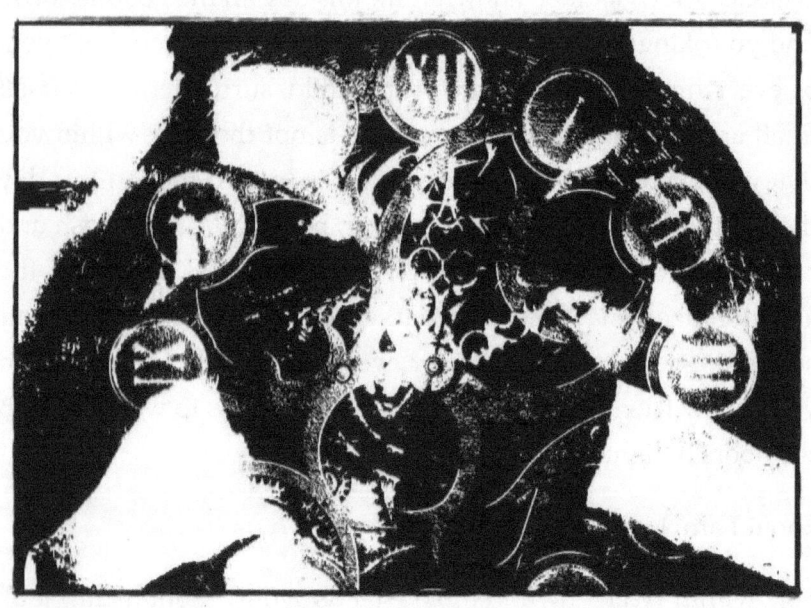

Chapter Five

The Telepathist's

Aldus and Rean soon found their way through the light, and towards a new pathway leading them in the direction of three tall white lighted forms', they looked like three men standing in front of a light.

"Who are they Aldus?"

"There known as the telepathist's, very strong and wise beings that will show you many new ways of thinking, this is as far as I can go with you Rean, you must go to them and trust them as you did me, my time as your guide is at the end, so now go Rean."

"Oh Aldus, I thank you from my heart for your kind wisdom and will follow them as I did you... thank you and goodbye my friend."

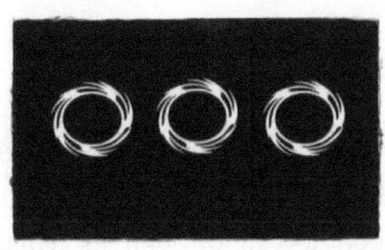

Rean was told by Aldus to stretch out his hand as a sign of conventionalism and willing to go with them without any kind of struggle, for he would have to be willing to go with them and allow the telepathists to show him the new way, and without consent this would not be allowed.

A hand held out ready for his next part of the journey, and what would be of Aldus?

"Welcome Rean we know so much about you, come with us we have so much to show you."

"You know of me?" Rean replied with haste

"Yes, it is known that the traveller is on his way and that the time was here to show him the way"

Path be new, path be true, show him the way through all that will see him done, till lighted night shine all that is bright, forthwith is the breath of beating heart new, only knowing will see him true. As we stand to breathe all within you, forever and proper shall find this day of innovative thinking, the way, we… of that will travel within your mind true.

Oh beautiful light show him this day, for the opening from our hearts cannot be told unless he can see through your eyes, may we not hurt the blood flowing through his veins.

Oh, let this day find its way to thy servant of knowing, the knowing will find everything within and grow towards the innovative inside the one who opens within, hold me now, and hold all that is for you, this second of this day is so important to you. First light in hand to hand is here we stand, in love and sight is how we will lift in our flight, for too long has man gone so wrong, in war and pain feeding the greed of anger and spite, growing in to the negative creeping monster, only to collapse into a defeated heap, leaving the suffering with corpses deep.

One should know where all went wrong, and stop the insanity before all has gone, listen to what will be said, pay attention to every word said, help stop the innocent falling to their death, for years and years so many have died, within living their full life, all because of greed and hate, don't let it happen ever again. Life on your world is falling fast as memories of war live on only to feed more and more.

The telepaths spoke in harmony "we have been observing the living of many years now, hiding in your time pieces, tick, tick, makes the sound though we here everything every sound every word that was spoken, recorded within our minds, a living nightmare of mankind, that is what has been spoken about your

47

living kind, it is essential that we try and help you stop this madness before all is lost."

"I am willing to do anything I can, I hate all the darkness that has found my kind, please, yes, please do help me find a way, I am ready for whatever you see fit for me." Rean replied

The telepathist's showed Rean into a large hall, this hall was filled with what could only be described as large monumental slabs with engravings imbedded in them, it was colossal, like something Rean had never seen before, his emotions where overcome and he fell to the floor.

Crying out "oh, this is so beautiful... I am lost in adoration and my stillness finds this hall as I am, please forgives me, I cannot help myself."

Tears of love fall to the hard cold floor, as they smash into the cold, the tears turn into senses of glass, finding their way and dissolving into the air.

"Rean do not worry yourself of showing your true feelings, no one can hide their true humanity within these walls in this hall, it is known as the halls of truth, and the knowing will find you."

Rean stud back up and showed his love lightened eyes, he tried to pull himself together. "Listen Rean, listen to what we have to tell you, for on this day you will see the writings in front of you and what will be spoken will be kept inside forever, now look to your   first   white   slab"

Rean turned his head to the right and looked directly towards the first slab, resonating from the white slab was a magnificent glow to meet his eyes. "Oh, it's astonishing, it's too much to take in" Rean replied in a panic of stimulation

"Do not worry Rean; you would not be normal if all this did not affect you"

The telepathist's pointed to the first symbol on the slab,

"That is the showing"

It reads,

Follow me now into the light and you shall see the truth of living, hold this breath in your heart and find the beginning from all that was and will be in front of you, your tomorrow is the answer.

Know yourself, and do love your brother and sister, the giving shall follow all within you, oh, this is forever, this is within you, so be true

Follow what you believe though don't hurt your brother nor your sister, they are the living body of everything around you, and what we do echoes around everywhere, oh beautiful everything shining around you, listen to the world sing, do not worry your mind with war and greed, the fruits of living and be wonderfully free, freeing the mind of hate and greed is what you will become and see the all new living around you.

Rean looked at the telepathist's and said, "this is making sense, I always knew of such wonderful words though I have just been limited within my owe head, not paying any attention to what could be and what was happening around me."

"Yes Rean we sometimes do not see the reality and let our misguiding's take over our way of thinking, though we can find our way back from this place, as long as our hearts are beating, our tomorrow can be the day to start a new and find the courage within to start our new way of thinking."

Ascending lights found Rean's eyes falling towards something on the floor in the hall.

He called out "what is this?"

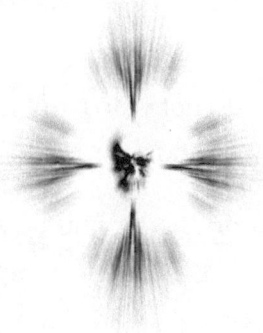

The telepathist's replied

"This is the symbol of the skull warper"

"The skull warper?" … Rean gasped

"This symbol is a significant part of thinking within the new way, though there are many new ways of thinking, the way of the skull warper are more useful to your way of knowing."

"It is hypnotic" Rean replied

"And rightly so Rean, it has many powers, and has been said to hold the one true authority on the one and only key philosophy"

The telepathist's read from an ancient script

Follow me not, for I do not live within your world, I do not breathe your air nor feed on your fruit, though I know why you are, and why it is that everything lives in this light.

Many of us shall seek and not find, though some will seek and become all new.

This passenger of light, do not worry thy mind, for on this day it has been said that one will find.

Let in that light as you do the air you breathe, follow your new beating   heart   towards   your   temple   of   the   true.

Shall we not judge this opened eyed child of the new world, though to let in love and dance within the celebrations of life.

Let it be known on this day, this wonderful sun lighted blessed day, that we shall let out the negative and find new positive within even the darkest of haze.

Overcoming our enemy's with not death or the power of war, though the use of inner love and finds the light within their hearts and talk within.

This perceptive on the new positive shall overcome any such power of negative death, for the new way shall find its light and see within all darkness.

Show thy self, stand within and become all new, all over everything ascending love towards positive skies within love and power of the mind.

Thy shine will light a thousand eyes, thy mind will enrich a million hearts, thy voices shall touch everything living becoming the all ascending powerful true.

As we stand together in flesh and bone, what is it that we see? What do we feel within, is voice the only true way to communicate? No, I tell you on this day we shall show you how we really see and talk through our mind and heart.

For this is the factual way of communicating, when we talk through voice this can separate us in the use of language, the indifference between you and me shall not come from this infected way of speech.

If you have the mind to follow and be true step within me and we shall find reasoning in togetherness and become one within the living.

Stand within towards this all new way of living.

So many have fallen, so many have killed for power and greed, if we don't come together and act strait away, then my friend all shall be lost forever and within our time.

Command this new way within your knowing and seek within this wanting, this necessary light needs your heart beat. This outside you are is not living.

Ascending with love finds you,

The all embodiment within light,

From this supreme feeling come within,

Finding this reason,

This fruit from your heart,

All seeing,

Everywhere,

Standing towards the everything,

Calling out truth,

Seek thy love within,

Show this to my brother and sister,

And we shall overcome the darkness,

With ever ascending love,

Within the light,

Travelling through time,

In love and rime,

From eye to eye,

The seekers path has been wrote,

Know thy destiny,

Touch this everything within you,

You to me and I will become truth,

Emending our ways from all darkened days,

When this light touches your face,

Is it not for wanting to find love in replace?

So hold this tight within your heart,

We shall begin our new passage within,

Hold this all destiny is depending on you.

We shall begin

This beautiful within, shall it not be starved of love no longer, shall the slowing of darkened misery blue forget its way upon you, and to only find a new... that shall be said, you

So let this love hold you strong, and we shall never do thy wrong, as morning finds its light my words will hold you forever in the might.

Ready for any such battle ahead, standing strong within the living dead, for our journey has just begun and we shall stand tall within love and truth so that nothing can go wrong.

The every reason of heart shall never pull us apart; this love that grows shall fight our entire never ending days. Caressing the lighting ways and speak out to many new all-around living new born witnesses towards the new days of thinking, of the sun blessed true.

Now we shall stand together and listen to what we shall do, let in thy light, let in thy love, become me as I become you, for our today has already started something so wonderful.

Stand within the skull and see if you're the one that shall be true, this shall be said that on this day,

This,

Is,

All we ask of you.

Chapter Six

The four

Towards the shifts of light found Rean's face staring upwards at the last slab on the halls gigantic wall, engraved wordings found his eyes; Rean's interpretation was somewhat obtuse as the expressions found him uneasy.

"Don't you worry yourself my friend, I was the same when I first viewed the engraved scriptures" sounded from a distant a comforting voice

Rean turned quickly with a question within his eyes, "who was that, show yourself, and be seen.

From the distance a tall friendly face appeared, "why that was me, my name is Saros; I am one of the four."

"Forgive me sir, I do not know of the four?

"We are named the four because of the ways of life, and we were given the undertaking to be your bodyguards, we have trained for many years in countless ways of protection, so you can count on our last breath of loyalty, to you and the path." Sounded Saros

"Come with me know my friend, and I will introduce you to the others."

Rean replied, "I guess I have to trust you also Saros, I have travelled this far and chanced on some interesting characters, they have been most helpful in the ways of my finding the path, so yes Saros, I will follow you."

Saros smiled and they set away towards a long tall doorway, while walking towards the doorway Rean asked Saros where the telepathist's had gone to, he told Rean that they was just a small part of this vast journey he was entering and that they was most grateful to have been part of his way.

From the towering doorway they stepped away onto a pathway leading them out within a vast landscape, this wasn't anything like Rean's living world; it was a terrifying and difficult part of the path. Saros walked Rean to a vast opening and said,

"Rean… this is our sleeper"

"Sleeper, what is that?" Rean pulled back his shoulders and asked.

"Why this is the way we travel my friend" replied Saros

Saros touch the air with his hand, the air started to go still to the sound of breathing songs from the lighted ever guided notes from the sky's, the sound was hauntingly beautiful.

While listening to the vibrating echoes Saros pushed an opening with the air, from this was a sphere, Saros told Rean to follow him into the sphere, as first stepped Saros then to follow the ever captivated Rean.

"This is amazing." Gasped Rean

"Ah… yes Rean, this is a remarkable traveling sleeper, it will take us safely to Diehemadgass, where the other of the four stand."

Saros pushed down his hand and the opening in the sleeper closed, he asked Rean to sit on a small red woven blanket while Saros held out his hand and closed his eyes, the sphere started to lift from the dusted ground, within seconds Rean and Saros where shifting through the deep blue skies.

Towards the middle I find you

Know see this traveling sphere

Within the air we go

To another land we travel

As I touch you air, oh beautiful air

Free us within your grasp

And guide us to your heart

Where we shall find the others

And our journey we shall start

Towards Diehemadgass Rean and Saros travel

Far past the mountains they flew with ease within the sleeper nothing could see them, when the sleeper fly's within the air, the sleeper becomes the air, becoming invisible to any sneaky seeing eyes that may want to attack such a moving object.

For the sleeper was crafted by the people of Diehemadgass, a very skilled craftsman was behind such a craft as the sleeper, from many years of inventing became this craft, only known to the few and a sworn secret, sworn to the heart of everything the all-powerful everything. Saros held up his arm and spoke out, "Now see me air of Diehemadgass, hold thy sleeper towards the gates of thy heart and show the air to follow us into the path of our all-powerful everything, into our love we travel, towards our land that is Diehemadgass, that land of truth, hidden deep within the our entire life, as we stand with you lighted sky's show us to thy hearted gaze, for on this day I bring Rean to thy beating heart."

The sky guided the sleeper towards a large plantation of trees, well what looked like trees, though they were just used as a camouflage from any unwanted visitors, they glided effortlessly towards the gates of Diehemadgass.

"So Rean, hear we are welcome to Diehemadgass." Saros called out.

They fell slowly towards the ground, Saros opened the door of the sleeper, a cheer found Rean and Saros, the people of Diehemadgass where standing towards Rean clapping and cheering out,

"Look, look its Rean; it's really him it's really him"

"Hurray for our descendant of the light, he will save us, he will save us, I just know it, hurray for Rean" came from the crowd.

Then a new voice found Rean's ears, "Now, now, let him in, I know you're all excited about see Rean though let him into Diehemadgass, into our hearts he belongs yes, though let him in, now be on your way my good citizens of Diehemadgass."

With that the crowd disbursed and within the departing happy faces was three persons standing tall, they started to walk slowly towards Rean, Looking up and down at him, every second a step closer. Rean could hear one of them speak,

"So that's Rean, finally we get to meet him after all these years we finally get to talk to him and live our destiny"

Saros turned to Rean a said, "these are the other part of me, my brothers we shall protect you we shall serve you until our last breath, Rean please let me introduce my brothers."

Saros turned to the approaching three and haled, "welcome my brothers, welcome on the glorious day, this is Rean, my brothers show him your love."

A voice first came from Jar,

"You are most welcome my friend."

Then from that came the voice of Hemessean,

"Welcome to Diehemadgass Rean."

Rean could not but stair at Hemessean; she was a vision of beauty. Then came the voice of Frestro the last of the three,

"Good day to you sir, it is so wonderful to see you, so wonderful."

Then came back the Voice of Saros, "Rean... we are the four, we will protect you, we will follow you, we are your arms, your legs, we live in your beating heart, and it is our duty and pleasure to walk with you.

Jar, Frestro, Hemessean and Saros bowed down to Rean and all pronounced,

"We the four, shall honour and protect you, our light is your light, our breath is your breath, we will live and sleep beside you."

They walked with Rean to his new chambers where they all would live and work with Rean, they had a lot of work to do, Rean knew what he wanted to achieve though did not know how, the four would guide him and help him become stronger in his body and mind, help Rean find his true self and become the everything within all opened light holding life within.

This would be a long journey in front of Rean and he had to be at his best, he had so much to overcome, they would have to rebuild Rean's body, his mind would have to expand so that he could use his everything, once the four have shown Rean the way, the path shall open and all will see through Rean.

This expanse of the unknown, will be overcome and grow into the true, find its love and blossom towards everything, when all will come together. And start to live a new, towards this expanding light the four will overcome any of Rean's darkness and show him the light.

Towards the ever clear new

Finds new sight with such a fight

To the fight of a broken wing

Do the four follow, day and night

Forever within their beating hearts

Will nothing pull them apart?

On this day they all stand

Hand in hand

To show Rean his way

Finding everything within to start the new day

As they walk towards his light

A journey will find his way

To the path

To the path

Is his only way

"I suppose you're feeling very tired Rean, Let me take you to where we rest our heads" said Hemessean.

"Yes, though with everything I don't want to sleep" replied Rean.

"I do understand Rean, it must all be very exciting for your mind to take in at this point, though you must rest, it is very important for your mind, we will start working on you tomorrow, so you will need all your strength, trust me sleep, and I will see you tomorrow. "Rean looked into Hemessean's eyes, his heart started to race, he thought to himself,

"How wonderful, what beauty lives in this person."

Hemessean

Hemessean gently touches Rean's chest and say's,

"Goodnight my friend"

She keeps her hand firmly pressed on his chest and say's,

"Your heart beats so fast"

Rean blushes smiles and shirks off to lay down, Hemessean walks away into the night,

"Sleep well my beating heart."

Rean enters his chamber and fall's face first on his bed. It seems like just a second rest and a shout comes from outside,

"Rean are you ready, it is time to start our work."

It was Jar kicking the door,

"Wake up Rean, we have much to do."

Rean shouted in a sleeping daze,

"Yes... ok, err... I will be out soon."

"We will meet you out side, hurry." shouted Jar

Rean had woken up and got his head together and was ready for the new day, though he did not know what to expect, he just made his way outside and hoped for the best.

"Hi Rean, good morning my friend, we hope you had a good night's sleep?" said Jar.

"Yes thanks, it went so fast, though I am ready for this day's work, show me what I must do" Rean nervously replied.

The four and Rean set away towards the great training hut on the mountains of Diehemadgass; this would be a short journey, though they had to travel in the sleeper. They set away into the sky and soon arrived at the hut on top of the mountain.

"This way Rean we have much to do though first we must eat" shouted out Saros.

They all sat around an old wooden table with wooden boll's full of a strange looking food, looked similar to soup.

"This will do us good for the day; it's full of energy and will give us much strength." Smiled Frestro

Rean tasted the strange looking soup and thought it was delicious.

"That was nice, what is inside this strange looking dish?" said Rean. Saros replied,

"Your best not knowing Rean just enjoy the taste."

"Now Rean come with us, it is time to start our training," said Saros.

They showed Rean into a hut, and all sat down on an old wooden floor.

Saros looked at Rean and said,

"As we stand here with you your training begins, you must always listen and follow what we say, to every seconds thought, you must understand we will show you well, and you will no doubt listen and learn well, so far you have listened well and understood what is expected of you. We are all hear today for one reason and that is to help Rean see his path and find his way,"

"Look at me Rean, look into my eyes and tell me what you feel within" said Saros.

Rean looked deep into his eyes; all of a sudden he could feel a connection though did not know why.

Saros asked Rean to stand and look as he asked Jar to come and stand next to him, Saros closed his eyes and told Jar to try to attack him, Jar pull out a large strange looking bladed weapon and ran straight at Saros, Jar didn't even get to touch Saros, not a chance, he was thrown to the other side of the hut.

Jar was fine he knew what to expect and how to fall, you see Saros was using his energies from his mind combined with his physical strength, the way of mind and body, Saros made himself unharmed and protected using his mind to control the worlds energies combined with his own.

"So you see Rean, we really are all connected with everything around us, and we can tune in to what is around us and become the air" said Saros.

"Yes, like we did when we were in the sleeper." Replied Rean

They all applauded Rean.

"Yes, yes, well done my friend, you see I knew you were paying attention, very well done my friend, he certainly is the gifted one." Happily replied Saros

Rean was asked to stand with the four in a circle, with their eyes closed and their arms held towards the sky, Saros called out to the light,

"On this day let it be known we are now strong, for we are together, to all and above we invite Rean our friend of the light to come with us and find his path, oh energies find him like you did us, find him, find him." Called Saros

Enter the light

Find reason new

Consequence for the darkened sky's

For this day was the way of new light

Holding true

Within this bright

Holds such love for the new world

Send me not thy pain

Out to the end we shall follow

Thy seeker talks with this day

From distance now come to us and find our hearts

Beating towards the lighted ended view

Send us towards

The circle was lighted in the centre became the energy presence and said.

"we give you your true gift, we hold you within the everything new and around you, we shall enter though thy friend and then through your body, with flesh and bone we shall find thy heart beating through your own, to the lighted day this will find your way, be truthful and see, love and live for the energy new will find you, the ever shining new inside you."

From the presence a light found the circle of friends and gave Rean his new life energy and wisdom that he would need for the future.

Stand now

Stand strong

Look into the air

An see everything new

Oh, this beautiful you

Emending all that was sad

To ever changing bliss

All around and be said

Never to cry now son

Lay thy head on this light

And stand true

With thy friends you're so strong

Ever so new they will stand with you

Take care of your love

And thy will never go wrong

Touch your heart and feel this day

We are you new born mind

The eyes from everlasting heart

Thy slay within the darkened way

Should not be taken away

Though used in a new way

When you feel me with you

Oh, so true, new life with you

With you, now with you

Thy hand is strong

Trust and nothing with go wrong

The light past over Rean and the others and touch them all, though more so Rean, he was now a full part of them and everything around him, with this he could now understand and see such wonderful things that he could have never dream of before, this was truly an amazing day for Rean, finally he had become his real self and overcome all his negatives.

Rean felt amazing all his body was so alive, like he had never felt be for, his brain was completely awakened, he was so Hungary for knowledge.

They had to go to the time of perceptive a place where Rean could read an learn, this was like some kind of library, though a time library, where time could stand still and Rean would read many books and listen to numerous ways of wisdom's teaching him, feeding his brain with everything he wanted, and time would stay still while doing so, it would be like a blink of an eye and Rean would have all the knowledge he needed, a truly magnificent time library was just what he needed to feed this new brain.

"This hunger, I want to learn about everything, I want to do well, I feel so strong, and I feel wonderful" shouted Rean

They showed Rean to the time Library and let him feed upon the knowledge's of time, he would be so strong with all this within his new mind; the light would have a new day when all would be done.

Rean nourished on everything, his hunger was strong, and how he encouraged the knowledge to fill his head and body.

" I feel so strong now, I feel like I can do anything I want, all this is with me know and I shall do good things, I want to find my way into the path and having all this within me will help me see and become the new that I always wanted too."

"To find my way within the new, to see through the darkness and show this light that is with us all, though shaded from most bye the thing that we should love."

While in the time library Rean found a script, and it read,

Show me your openness

And become this life

Away with thy darkened stain

Thy blood will live true

Within everything around you

Go to thy friend and listen

Stand to thy air

And feel your new day

Your strength is guided

Towards you, within everything new

And you're the strength that will save all

Be that light, be that new, be you

All ascending found his heart, body and mind Rean was now strong and ready for anything.

The sky open with new light towards the high glades that found a way to new found love, within all ascending light opened towards Rean's beating heart.

Saros finds Rean sitting on a wall next to the time Library, Rean was gazing into space; He looked like new, something amazing had happened to his body and mind. Rean was like a new man ready for anything, or was he?

Saros could see Rean was very pleased with himself; Saros didn't want to spoil his day, though he had to tell him. Though he wasn't shore how to tell him. Saros pondered with himself as he walked nearer and nearer.

As Saros found Rean he looked into Rean's eye's and said,

"Rean, my friend I have woeful news, and I am so sorry to have to welcome you with this saddened greeting, It's…"

Rean called out "Oh, my wonderful friend I already know."

"How could this be, you have been totally alone, how could you know?" said Saros folding his arms.

"You see Saros, I just know, I felt the passing of Aldus, the soul of Aldus's tribe came to me a few weeks ago and explained everything, so you see I felt the passing of my friend, I am now connected with the air, with this ever expanding everything, Saros I have become myself complete, on this day I stand in front of my good friend Saros and say to him that all is well, we shall overcome the darkness and work together and overcome this melancholy by holding out our arms and hearts to the living world, for Aldus is now the air and all around us, so do not be saddened my good friend, he is with us all."

"I could not believe what happened; it is good that you know Rean, I am at ease now we have talked." Said Saros

Aldus was a strong part of the UConn tribe, he was one of Rean's guides and did a great job, though the negative nasty's found him, he was court off guard, they crept upon his good nature, he was unsuspecting, poor Aldus. The negative nasty's, they stand among you as a friend, then when you're unaware they take you away. A negative nasty is the worst; they have been described like having a draining sole machine plugged in you at all time, posing as a friend and telling you how sad they are, only draining you of everything you have until they see that you have no more and take you away, the negative nasty's, true monsters, keep a lookout for them they live with you too.

Aldus did not stand a chance; they drained him from everything he had.

"Saros, we have been summoned to the Aldus's tribe to say goodbye and also to look out to make shore their isn't any more of the negative nasty's living with them, let us go and find the others it is time for us to travel my friend." Said Rean

"Yes Rean, we should go and see if we can find that negative nasty, that scum of the living world, to take away such a wonderful life is deeply saddening my friend, let us go and gather the rest of the four, I am shore they will also be keen to seek the negative nasty's out." Said Saros

They set away back to Diehemadgass to meet up with the rest of the four, traveling swiftly through the skies.

Towards and above

To find a reasoning from the darkness

Looking inwards feeling the loss

Stand they will with strength in their hearts

Nothing will be stronger than the one's of the light

They shall find all that is true

Find out the negative nasty around you

For you should look all around

Their hiding as friends

Only to take you away

Look out

Look out the negative nasty is about

Stand thy strong as Rean and the four

Will seek him out

With the knowing of the negative might

For this strength is so very strong

Though they know just what to look out for

The deepest or darkness isn't always dressed in black

Their ready to take you at any time

When you're at your uttermost fragile state

The negative nasty sits and waits

"Welcome back Rean and Saros, we have missed you both, come and have something to eat." Shouted out Jar, in a welcomed tone

"Don't tell me, more strange soup?" replied Rean

Jar and Saros let out a smile looked at each other and shouted out "oh, Rean we are truly gladdened of your return."

They set back into the hut where Frestro and Hemessean were preparing food; the atmosphere had sadness though a gentle calm was holding everything together.

Together they sat eating the strange soup and all was good,

"So Rean, what should we do next, what is it we have to do?" said Jar

"My friends, after our meal we shall go to the sleeper and travel to the UConn tribe, we have been asking to go and make sure all is well, keep a lookout for that negative nasty." Replied Rean

"I hate them with a passion!" called out Frestro,

"They give me the creeps."

"What is the plan Rean?" asked Saros

"When we arrive, I and Hemessean will welcome the new tribe's leader, I expect this will be Untay and Saros, Jar and Frestro you will go among the crowds, and you will all need your seekers on."   Replied   Rean

A seeker is a suit made to discover the negative nasty, it's attached to your heart, the suit is made just for you and only you can operate it. Once it becomes in near contact with a negative nasty the suit starts a trigger telling the suits that they are around.

"Dear friends if any of you find a negative nasty do not attempt to reach them without the others, we are so much stronger together, it would be suicide to try and catch it alone, do you all understand?" said Rean

They all replied, "Yes Rean, We understand, you have our faith and we shall follow and serve you."

"Good, this is good; we understand each other, now let us finish this strange soup, and then we are on our way."

They finished their meal and gathered everything they needed for the journey ahead, they knew that it would be no easy task to find such a thing as the negative nasty, as they are very strong and clever dark creatures, they have their eyes gouged out when they first arrive in this world, because they could not stand to see any kind of good, love to them is like punching them in the face with a steal knuckle duster, they made them self's look like humans, their very good at that, they get into your being and recognise what makes you feel trusting and easy then become just that. Though if you would see the Negative nasty real form and presence, you would be terrified, a truly hideous monster.

83

The only known photo of a negative nasty

They set away in their sleeper towards the tribe, ever so high and fast, becoming the air traveling within this everything so quietly on   a   sound

They went deep and far into the sky's

Towards the people of the UConn tribe to find the darkened one, seek him and let them be new, let the people find their new leader with love and hope, though they had to be strong as it was a difficult task that was ahead of them.

They were strong and knew what to do, so everything was going to plan, they went deep and far into the sky's.

Chapter Seven

Into The UConn Tribe

The twisting of this lighted day had found the sleeper falling from the highest of skies, towards an opening that found them drifting with the UConn tribe, standing to meet them was the new leader Untay, and hid guards.

"Welcome my friends, we are so pleased to see you all, we thank you from our heart, that you would come and help us at our time of need, this is welcomed with open arms, we say welcome please follow us, we shall show you to your rooms where you will stay until you see fit to leave us my friends, follow us."

They followed Untay and his guards within the centre of UConn, it was a bright dwelling with many of the tribe's people going this way and that way, all around was life, a truly lively habitation. The accommodation was held inside an enormous stone temple built with love and great skill, it has been said that the temple of UConn took many years of craftsmanship to finish, inside of the temple the UConn tribe lived safe and well in peace and tranquillity.

Rean and the others were taken to a large spacious dwelling with everything they would need for their task at hand.

"We thank you Untay, this is most welcomed, a truly amazing place, we are humbled at such generosity." Said Rean

"Please take your time my friends and familiarize yourselves with your new surroundings, I give you the entire key, this will open a door with our temple." Said Untay

Untay held out a long golden key and placed it into Rean's hand, once the key found Rean, it dissolved into Rean's hand and became a part of him. Rean thanked Untay and asked the four to form a circle.

"As I stand with you I give you all my power to see, and use the key gifted to me, hold it within your heart, we will need it from time to time, to help us find the negative nasty if there is one around us we shall send it on its way, put on your suits and we shall be on our way." Said Rean

They all suited up and were ready for their task ahead of them, with beating hearts and eager minds they set off into the working of the Temple.

Rean set off with Hemessean and shouted out to the others, "remember if you detect a negative nasty wait until we are all together, and go well my friends."

Jar, Frestro and Saros went within the people, Rean and Hemessean set off the other way deep under the Temple's underground tunnels. They walked down into the darkness; though it was dark the feeling was mindfulness with light in their minds.

Hemessean walked in front of Rean holding out her hand, from Hemessean's hand came light, not too blinding just enough to see from.

"Is this okay Rean, can you see well enough?"

"Yes thank you Hemessean, we shall go right down into the dwellings, I think that would be a great place to start." Replied Rean

They carried on deep into the darkness until they arrive at the deepest part of the underground temple.

"What is that?" whispered Hemessean, standing closer to Rean

Rean held Hemessean's arm and calmly said, "That's just the guard, he's asleep, and I think he's snoring."

Hemessean replied "so that's the what I could hear, I'm sorry Rean I feel a bit jumpy down here, I'm never much use in the dark, I need the light, dam this darken hole."

"I know where you're coming from Hemessean this place is creepy, very creepy." Said Rean

They stud in the centre of the deepest part of the darkness and held hands to make a circle of light.

Rean whispered towards the tiny shimmers of light bouncing off the cold water dripping down from stone walls,

"Oh, light I seek you, hold thy mind strong, we stand here today where others have done wrong, I ask my light to find the evil within these walls, and show us the way, do not cry tonight thy darkened one, nor you oh forgotten soul, I call you know, I call from the light, where are you, where do thy dwell with thy misery, don't hide from my heart tonight come with me to show yourself, come talk to the my mind, show yourself." Rean called out towards the light

They stud in a circle surrounded in darkness.

Whispers started to arrive,

Utterings,

I can smell your human flesh

The stench makes me sick

Your goodness is so true

What's thy name?

I want to take you far away

Into darkness misery new

Where pain and sadness

Finds all like you

You sickening living stench

You dare to call on me

Why I should take you now into never-ending darkness

Your stupidity amazes me

Never before have I been summoned in this way

Who stands before me?

Who shall I slay today?

"Show yourself, oh, darkened one, show thy self o darkened scum of all that is evil." Called out Rean

Rean quickly closed his eyes and summoned the others to join him and Hemessean, "come quickly... quickly my friend, it is here."

Jar, Saros and Frestro teleported themselves to Rean and Hemessean, they formed a superior circle. Nothing could break this power where too vibrant, in that darkened hold where the upmost of power from all light of hearts, the others kept quiet as they knew Rean was in total control.

"Again and again Rean called out, "show thy self, show thy self oh, you negative nasty, yes… we know what you are, come show your hideous mass of darkened evil, show yourself."

A forming dark greyed cloud found the underground circle, hovering above them was a storm of evil, yes; it was the negative nasty, right above their heads.

"We have come for you, we are too strong for you and you know it, your time is up, how dare you take my friend Aldus, he was a remarkable light with this world, though now you will pay for this." Shouted Rean towards the ever growing cloud

The negative nasty was so angry, Rean had summoned this mass of evil and it had never before felt such power, knowing its time was nearly up the clouded mass spoke out,

"You're so strong

Where did you come from?

Never in my darkened day

Have I felt such power of the light?

So my time is soon up

When you show me the light

And this cloud will be no more

Death for me is soon I know

Though when I go I shall leave you the sickness

For into one of you shall fall the fever of hell

One of my favourite of smells

So go ahead kill me now

Show me this light and do me good

I'm ready for your fight."

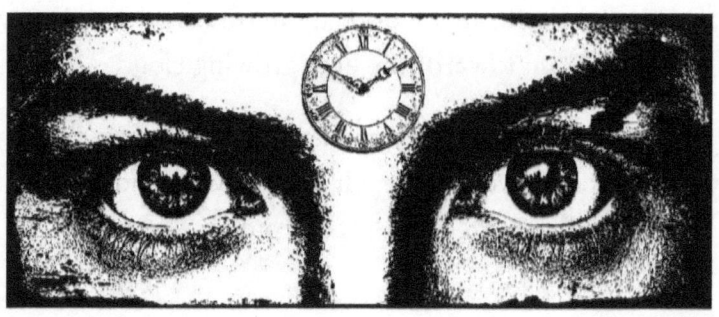

Rean opened his eyes and a blinding light found the darkened cloud, it was so bright. Screams of the most horrid echoed around them all, shakes with energies of beating light traveling through them all. The power was too strong for the negative nasty; Rean had referred back to one of the books in the time library saying *"if you show goodness in abundance to true evil, the light will always win."* And it worked.

He had become so sick just like the negative nasty predicted, Frestro was very sick and they had to get him out of their and back in the light so that Rean and the others could sort out what they could do for Frestro, it was the most of all evils that had entered his body, they had to get out and quick.

"Come my friends, let us get out of here; we shall teleport back into the light."

Frestro lay so sick in the shelter given by the UConn tribe, shivering   and   muttering.

Untay entered the shelter and spoke out,

"Oh, my friends I am so sorry for this, I feel it is our fault that this has happened, and I am so sorry, so very sorry."

He sat next to Frestro and tried to comfort him, Rean new that Frestro was done for; it was just a matter of time before he passed away, and it was a tall price to pay though it had to be done.

Within a few days Frestro passed away and they pay their respects to his soul, deep down he was still with them, not in body though in there light.

Within this light he fly's free

With his friends ready for the next day

Be free now my friend

You helped rid of the evil

We will never forget you

Be still now

Light thy sky

Rean had to find strength for him and the others, the mood was low, though Rean new that time would help and things would never be the same without Frestro, though time would heal their hearts. It was a tall price to pay to lose such a good friend though they had to get rid of the negative nasty; it was becoming too strong and needed to be killed.

After a few weeks staying with the UConn tribe they were feeling stronger, the unit found new strength to carry on their way home. After their long journey back Rean told everyone to take a few weeks alone and find themselves, Rean new after a good rest everyone would feel better so that they could carry on with their journey towards the path.

A few weeks into the rest period Rean received a message from Hemessean, asking if he would like to meet up as she was missing him.

Rean was also missing Hemessean at that point but did not want to contact her in case she needed more time to repair herself, Rean was really happy that Hemessean had contacted him, so he wrote back saying it would be great to get together whenever Hemessean felt like meeting up.

A few days passed and Rean received a knock on the door, Rean walked to the door and opened it,

"Ah, Hemessean, welcome my friend."

"And it is good to see you too Rean, I have missed you."

Rean smiled back at Hemessean and said,

"You're looking well Hemessean."

Hemessean walked through the door way and gently passed by Rean's arm, a perfumed breeze hit Rean's nose. Rean loved that smell it made him feel at ease.

"So Rean, what have you been doing?" said Hemessean

"No doubt the same as you Hemessean, recharging and doing loads of thinking; it is great to see you."

Hemessean looked at Rean and said,

"Oh Rean, I have something to tell you, though I don't know how you're going to take it?"

"What is it Hemessean." Rean answered in a playful way

Hemessean walked closer to Rean and looked into his eyes and said,

"Oh, Rean after the death of our good friend Frestro, I have been doing a lot of deep thinking, and have decided that life is too short, and,"

She paused for a short moment,

"Well, what I'm trying to say to you is that I have feelings for you, not just for friendship, my heart wants more, please I don't want to say anything to upset you, though I know that we have felt more than just friendship in the past meetings."

Rean's heart started to beat; his hands became clammy, like he was back at school again.

Rean smiled and said,

"My dear Hemessean, I feel the same way."

With that Hemessean, walked towards Rean and kissed him, again and again they kissed each other.

"O Rean, I need this." Said Hemessean while caressing Rean's chest

Rean unclothed Hemessean and they both fell naked on the bed, making passionate love for hours till late into the knight, enjoying the pleasures of their new lustful attraction.

They lay together in their bed naked,

"Rean, that was amazing." Hemessean whispered in Rean's ear

Rean looked into Hemessean eyes and said,

"You are so beautiful; when we first met I felt something for you, I just knew something was going to happen between us, you have made my day, O Hemessean" They fell deep into sleep and awoke the next morning, making passionate love.

They eventually fell from their love nest and set out together, they were all summoned to the high council of Casszoolas.

Chapter Eight

The High Council of Casszoolas

The high council of Casszoolas was deep within the hills of Casszool, a very secret inhabitation, the dwelling of the almighty king of light; his name is Huzang, the all mighty king.

Touched by the light

Forever within your sight

This being shall live for the ever

So strong and bold

Many tall of the untold

They go to see him

In his kingdom strong

Where the next task will be set

Deep within the hill

Hidden away

Of only the chosen few to see

A true honour is the blessed that is

Soon they will see him

And see him they will

Strength will see

"It is good to see you all hear my friends." Shouts a high guard standing at the top of a large hall, surrounded by tables full of all kinds of people, from all over the worlds

"Please stand for the king, King Huzang, our head of all that is true, we stand with you." Shouted out the guard with pride echoing down the hall's

Everyone stud, and cheered for the king, A thousand voices echoed towards the king.

"We hold our arms out in care of our king, king Huzang." They called out.

"Welcome my good friends, it is wonderful to see everything hear on this day, I welcome you all with all my heart, and let it be known on this day that everyone inside these walls are my heart, and free in my mind, we are one."

"Let us eat and be merry on this day, feed well my friends." The king fell into his seat and stuffed his face with food and wine.

Rean, Hemessean, Jar and Saros where sitting together on the same long table enjoying their feed, when one of the guards came up the Rean and whispered in Rean's ear,

"The king would like to see you and the others, tomorrow, he and the high council have something to tell you all, for now enjoy your   food,   good   day   Rean."

The guard walked away and disappeared into the noise, the eating and drinking went on deep into the night, the next day soon dawned, Rean had told the others to meet him at the doors of the high council, and the next day had soon arrived and for some a little too soon.

"Oh, my head" squealed out Jar

"It serves you right Jar, you always over do things." Laughing out Hemessean, with a loving smile

They all laughed and waited to be summoned to see the high council, it was not long before, the guard stud above Rean and the others saying,

"Please follow me; it is time for you to address the high council of Casszoolas, please do not talk until asked, please follow me."

Rean and the others walked alongside each other towards the doors leading them into the courts of the high council, the large darken blackened wooden doors opened, with ease, Rean whispered to the others,

"Hold your chins up and walk with me."

They all stud in a line of four directly in front of the high council, a long table of the most significant persons of all and around, it was a truly monumental day, to be standing in front of such importance was not something that happened every day, the importance was deeply felt all around the different circles around the new lighted worlds.

It was time for the council to speak,

"Welcome Rean, Saros, Hemessean and welcome Jar, it has been said that you on this day should come to the high council of Casszoolas, as a matter of great importance, please stand with us and show yourself to the council, call out your name starting from Rean, do so now." Called out Ennin chief of all courts

Rean stepped forward and said,

"I Rean guardian of all light and love, protector of life stand among you with my unity to you the high council."

Saros was next to step forward,

"I Saros protector of Rean stand among you with my unity to you the high council."

Next was Hemessean to stand and say,

"I Hemessean protector of Rean stand among you with my unity to you the high council."

Then last to stand was the ever faithful Jar,

"I jar protector of Rean stand among you with my unity to you the high council."

They all stud tall together and bowed down in high opinion of the high council.

They waited for someone to speak out; it was the king, king Huzang,

"My good friends, I thank you for attending this meeting, first of all I want to say how sorry we were to hear of Frestro, he will be deeply missed." Called out the king

Rean felt tears coming, "no I must hold things together, and I must be strong."

The king spoke,

"On this day I send out our love, too you all and hope all your strength will grow into all your hearts, he will always be remembered, in his bravery, in his love and loyalty to the path of light, let it be the light from his life, now passed though still with us. Let him never be missed, for he lives as long as we do, too Frestro a courageous soul."

The king held out his arms and slowly lowered down his hands, with a symbol of the passing into light, this was a wonderful thing to do, Rean and the others where overcome with such respect to a fellow friend, they were so please the king to do that for their good friend, how wonderful.

"Now my friends we shall have to move out conversations too new matters, matters of extreme importance, for our world has grown darker and we have to come together on this day to talk about the protection of all and everything around us, this is the utmost of importance, time is not on or side, and let it be known I do not say this lightly."

The king bowed his eye brows and his head fell towards the table, and then stopped and he looked directly at Rean and the others and said,

"On this day I have the sad news of the ever growing knowledge those sightings of many of the hideous negative nasty's have come more and more common among our people."

The king stopped for a drink of water and carried on,

"our people, yes, it has become with each day that I hear about new sighting of the negative nasty's, we must stop them at any cost, this will no doubt, be a very difficult task for us all though we have to stand strong and stop them."

"I have asked you all to stand in front of me and I also ask for your help, we know you have the powers to kill and destroy these monsters of the dark, we have total faith of all your powers, so we stand with you on this day and say, please stand with us and fight for us against this evil shadow that travels through our kingdoms, what do you say protectors of the light, can you help rid us of such an evil might?"

Rean bowed down his head and replied,

"We are your servants of the light, yes sir, to our last breath, Yes sir,   we   shall."   Rean   proudly   replied.

The high council then began to whisper among their self's, sitting back and forth on their chairs, something at the utmost of importance was been discussed between them.

Rean whisper to Hemessean, "You look beautiful today." And smiled her way

"Why thank you Rean." Hemessean looking deep into Rean's eyes and blushing

They all waited for a reply from the high council, still whispers to them self's.

Ennin stud and spoke to Rean and the others, "we the high council of Casszoolas would like to thank all of you for your courage and we humbly welcome you into our hearts, it has been decided that you will be given total control of the capture and executions of the negative nasty's, we have nothing but the upmost contempt for this evil that has come upon our people and will be glad to see the back of such an evil manifestations."

Ennin paused for a short while and looked at the king, looked back towards Rean and the others and said,

"Dear friends this will not be an easy task, the consequences could be most terrible on you and all of our living kind, as you well know from your past meeting with the evil negative nasty, though this time it has become much stronger and has become more knowledgeable on the human mind, I don't understand how this happened though the negative nasty somehow entered the great time library."

Rean and the others gasped, while Ennin spoke out

"This is very worrying for us and our people, as they now know how we think, and how we live, they have everything on us, and all of our past history, they have since used all of this information and,"

She paused again, a tear fell from Ennin eye, and she pulled herself together and said,

"Well... they have been experimenting on some of their human prisoners."

A gasp came from Rean and the others,

"Yes... Experimenting on our friends, and they have been growing, and come up with a new horrific form of evil, this is not all information we have from a captured negative nasty we have in the secure cell deep underground, we first need Rean to question the evil scum, and see if you can get more information, as...I know the monster is hiding so much more from us."

"Yes, I have never known anyone capture a negative nasty before, though yes...I will do what I know is best high council, I will do my best." Rean looked up to the high council and replied.

"We don't have to tell you to be careful, though let it be known that this evil has become more that you have ever seen...felt before, though it does not have eyes, this evil can somehow see everything?...we do not understand how, be very observant while in its dark presence, we have it under constant guard, and it is surrounded by light of the all-powerful everything, so this one cannot move very fast, though be warned the evil filth has new things we don't understand and it is very good with its new powers...be careful Rean, You will visit the negative nasty tomorrow midday while there is the most strongest daylight." Replied Ennin

The high council all stud up and held their hands out to the air giving light from their hands, and said,

"For the light"

Rean and the others held their hands out to the air and replied,

"For the light"

Rean and the others walked out of the room, looking concerned of what was going to happen; only time could tell them the answer to that question. "We should all get some sleep, tomorrow will soon be on us and we have much to do, let us rest our heads tonight I will see you all in the morning early my friends." Said Rean

Hemessean walked back with Rean to his quarters, while the other also set off to their quarters paying good attention to Rean's words on getting a good night's sleep, with a nervous atmosphere in the air the night grew dark and morning soon arrived with the beautiful sound of the song of the sinning bird, little wing, the Little Wing was half bird and half human and had a voice like no other, made by the great inventor Lusan, a true artist.

Little Wing

Rean awoke and turned to Hemessean, he stared at Hemessean's beauty, in wonder and joy, Hemessean's eyes slowly opened and gazed at Rean with complete love towards him, truly a wonderful start to the day. Rean kissed Hemessean, and said

"I thank your life for showing me to this moment, this day I hold true, within my heart live the deepest of love for who I see, know and forever I shell adore you...Oh, my beautiful Hemessean, your Hemessean kissed Rean back and touched his chest gently while replying,

"Oh, Rean you're so wonderful, I don't know what I did before I found your heart, and may we never fall part."

They kissed and made first light love with the sound of little wing singing towards the ever clearing lighted skies. Midday soon arrived and they all met back at the doors of the high council, they did not know what would be ahead of them, the brave young things would stand tall towards to the tyranny of darkness.

"Did you get good rest Jar?" Said Rean

"Yes my friend, I soon fell away in the deepest of sleep, though it is strange how I never know my dreams?

"Maybe that is a good thing Jar." Replied Hemessean

Jar smile back to Hemessean and said,

"Yes maybe, maybe?"

With that a call from Ennin,

My world my heart beat."

"Rean, Hemessean, Jar and Saros, welcome we must go straight to the negative nasty at haste, please follow me."

They set away deep down into the very depths of Casszoolas, where only evil could be, it was dark deep to the bone with the sounds and echoes of the evil cries of the negative nasty the closer they became the louder the terrifying cries became, echoing all around them... deeper and deeper they walked into the darkened hole of imprisonment, for only the most evil where put.

"Rean, please you must remember that this negative nasty is far more evil in its powers than the last one you encountered, so please be very careful my friend." Said Ennin

"Yes, I do understand Ennin, I shall and have understood everything from your wise words from yesterday, and I am completely aware of its powers, don't forget I also have studied in the time library, so I am ready for this encounter of evil, I do not take lightly to such evil presence and would never think that I am immortal, I care for this gift I have...my life I so cherished to me, and for this I will go easy with my courage and this evil that I will visit shall know thy power, for the power of thy light is ever so strong, and I am never going to let any form of evil offend this." Replied Rean

Eventually they found the deep strong hold that was the prison that held the evil negative nasty, such an evil foreboding presence found them, though they were ready for what was to be done, because the negative nasty was heavily guarded and could not move that much, Rean had decided that he would go into the cell alone as it could not touch him, this would not have happened if the negative nasty was free, it would be so much more dangerous that way. Rean put his protective suit on, though he didn't think he needed the where his protective suit, it wasn't like the last time, this evil presence was under guard, though he did where it just to keep the others at ease, he was finally ready to go into the cell.

"Take care." they all said "Please look after yourself my love." shouted out Hemessean. "Open the sell door." Rean shouted to the guards.

The thunder of two layers of raw steel doors grinding together opened a blinding lighted cell; within the centre of the cell was a glass hovering cube unbreakable, inside was the evil negative nasty, angry, frustrated for been captured and very stubborn.

Rean stared into the glass cubed cell with a curiosity, as he had never really looked properly at the negative nasty, the last time he was with one was in battle and he didn't have much time to look at this pureness of evil. This was evil at its worst, shivers found his back as the negative nasty turned towards him and said,

"Who comes to me, who stands this human vomit?"

Rean looked straight at this and instantly remembered his good friend Frestro, he stud strong and replied,

"You talk of vomit, that is rich coming from pure filth, you sicken my heart, how dare you live you piece of waist, you sicken me, your nothing, hear me... nothing."

The negative nasty slowly turned his back to Rean and muttered,

"You know nothing, you're just human, the human can only do one thing, and that is dying."

Rean replied,

"Tell me evil, I hear your kind have been making plans of some kind?"

"why should I tell you anything, you will all soon find out, and find out you will, when the air grows thick and dark, time will stand still and death will come for you all, mark my words it is coming...human scum." Shouted the negative nasty

Rean looked down and said,

"Be still, your time is soon, tell me and I will make it fast...tell me!"

The cell started to go dark, with grey looms of clouds covering the Negative Nasty, with an uneasy feeling finding the room, slowly the clouds fell to the negative nasty's feet, revealing it holding something, and the negative nasty turned and held out the talking corpse of his good friend Frestro.

"Rean...Rean, it's me your good friend, soon it will all be over you're all going to die...your pain will be immense!" shouted out the dead talking corpse of Frestro.

Rean could not believe what he was seeing; right in front of him was Frestro, but then he stepped away and remembered how good at lying the negative nasty could be.

Still crying out was the corpse hanging from the arm of the negative nasty, Rean pulled himself together and shouted

"Be gone…be gone apparition, you're not my good friend, what I see in front of me is just an evil trick, be gone, evil, be gone."

With that the corpse disappeared, the negative nasty laughed at Rean,

"He was in so much pain before he died, did you know that." smiled out the negative nasty.

At that point Rean new there was nothing he could do here, and remembered from the literature from the time library, the best way to deal with the negative nasty, is for every negative he hits out at you, you should counterbalance it with a positive, Rean looked back at the negative nasty and said.

"I have such wonderful memories of my good friend and what I knew of Frestro is that he was so full of goodness, and I am thankful for every second of his friendship, what a beautiful…wonderful human being he was, he will always live on in my and all my friends memories, he was truly a treasured friend, so you may have taken his living form, though not our true living memories …no you can never do that."

The negative nasty trembled in his cell and let out a scream,

"You make me sick, now leave me, and go away…go away!"

Rean could do nothing more, he walked out and the massive steal doors slammed behind him; Ennin was waiting for Rean,

"My dear friend we are so sorry you had to see that! How did you do that without losing your mind?

With a tear in his eye Rean turned to Ennin and said,

"Oh…Ennin, the sadness I felt in that room, the loneliness, Oh my friend I would not wish that on anyone!, I knew it could never really be Frestro…I just remembered from the time library and held everything together."

Ennin looked into Rean's eye's and said,

"That was wonderful what you said back to that evil monster, truly magnificent."

"Remember for every negative can follow a stronger positive, and then the negative always falls." Rean replied with a smile

What became of the negative nasty, well…it lay in its own sadness within its own cell and fell into the lighted room, muttering and crying to its self until it gave up and passed away with no power in its saddened presence.

Always within light you will find a true form of love that can only feed the positives within life, no darkness can take everything away from our light, yes life can be taken from us, through self and through the control of others, though when memories of true friendships living on through the years and told to the new born, then no true friend ever dies.

Seek a light within your heart keep it lighted friend, keep it lighted, for the light is your strength, a strength that will carry you through your darkest time, your heart will follow you through the dark with the light deep inside your being, never lose thy light and hold your strength towards any form of darkness, for within the shadowed mind positives will always rise with the sun and become new within thy heart, show thy self to the light within, show thy love to friend in need, when beating heart finds you, show thy love and hold them with you, strength is within deep and forever are you.

Rean went to see the others, there was a meeting in the great public hall and many had gathered, to see the one's that would rid them of the evil that was surrounding their life's and they were interested in how they was going to do it.

For many years the people of Casszoolas lived a peaceful and joyful existence and to have such evil threating with them was most unwelcomed, so they was very relieved to know that Rean and the others had plans to destroy this evil presence among them, all they really wanted was to have a happy peaceful life they couldn't understand that is the very reason why the negative nasty wanted control over their life's, they wanted what the good people of Casszoolas has in abundance, the power of heart once manipulated could so easily be turned by the unknowing and made into the purest of evil, growing towards the   ultimate   darkened   supremacy.

Rean and the others had a fight on their hands and it wasn't going to be easy, this darkness was growing and they were the only hope.

Twisting towards the emptiness

Finds only the empty heart

Starved of love and torn apart

To find its way

Should be a life to show thy fear

Once found and among thy living

Will see thy way and open to all light

Find thy light oh darkened one

Hold this near

Thy words from true

Within holding mind

Steer him well

To the skies of bright

Where all will find lost friends

Tall and new

Remembering all new

Misted shadows will fall

Always to the sound of love

Fall to thy friendship glow

So let it be said

Pull thy through

Thy darkened time

And show him to light rime

Seeking all this now

Take nothing for granted

Hold thy friend near

Do not let him tumble

Towards the darkened hail

Hold thy strong

For your heart is thy light

Rean and the others had a day before the great meeting, a time to find new strength, to think, relax, and be ready for what would be asked of them, they knew it would be a difficult time so they was happy to have some time to relax.

"I will see you all tomorrow at the great hall." Rean called out to the others

"Yes, Rean, take care and relax my friend." Replied Jar

"Oh, I will my friend, and you all stay well, we have much to do and we will all need our strength." Rean replied

Rean and Hemessean set away towards their shelter,

"It is so beautiful today…do you see it Rean." Said Hemessean

"Oh yes Hemessean I have felt the sun on my back for a while now, we are fortunate to have such a wonderful day upon us, so let us enjoy this time and walk in the sunlight." Replied Rean with a smile

"How I love the heat of the sun on my back, let us not go straight to our shelter, let us set away to the open lands and soak in the suns glory, I noticed there is a lake where we can take a swim and relax." Said Hemessean

"What a wonderful idea, first we shall go to the market and gather something to eat, I am hungry and sick of that strange soup, yes let us go find some real food." Rean said

They gathered food and set away to the opening where trees sheltered a lake where they could take timeout and relax together. "Oh, Rean, this is wonderful, look at the trees there so alive and the lake is so calm, I'm going for a swim want to join me?" ask Hemessean

"Yes, that sounds delightful Hemessean," smiled Rean

Towards this love

Dancing together

On this day

The day of light

Let it be known

That love found their way

The kiss between two

Finding its way to thy dancing sight

Life is true within all this light

Nothing could stop thy way

Two forms embrace

Togetherness thy song is true

Lying next to each other Hemessean looks into Rean's eyes and says,

"My lover…my treasured friend, how did my life go without you next to my heart?"

"Oh, Hemessean, my love, I shall hold this thought and keep it forever, times like these make us rich, and we should hold on to such wonder."

"Yes, Rean I will hold on to this." Hemessean fell asleep on Rean

When they both woke up, they made their way back to their shelter and rested until the next day.

The light found the new day a yellowed haze on its path, holding true the start of its way, Rean and Hemessean awoke.

"Are you ready for today Rean?" asked Hemessean

"Yes Hemessean, I feel full of new energy and my head is well, and how are you for this new day my beautiful light?" replied Rean

"Oh, Rean, I am ready to follow you, I am with you towards the light we shall find the truth and become our new day, and for the rich sunlight shine will tell us to thy way towards a better life for all on this new day." Said Hemessean

"That is beautiful Hemessean, true words my love, we are the blessed to have been given lungs to inhale in this sun lighted air, let it show us the all truthful way, Oh light, light of today let it hold thy friends, and show us truth, hold us with strength, hold thy friend, hold me, Oh sun lighted skies hold us new, for we shall serve you true." Called out Rean

The skies kept shining, blossoming with opaque yellows allowing the sandy tans of tender orange to mix with the whites, finding a sun light dance within its skies.

This new ever essence day started a new with such beauty though the cloud would soon be turned and they both knew what was ahead, this would be a test for their hearts, for everything they had become.

Rean and Hemessean set away to the great public hall, a giant of a holding, where many where gathering, the sounds of many voices talking over each other, shouting, loud, noisy, ever so busy, more and more people filled the great public halls... truly an immense gathering, so many people.

"I didn't know that so many people would be coming to this meeting, it is very exciting." shouted out Hemessean to Rean

"Yes Hemessean, we should keep together, look other there...its Saros and Jar, let us go and greet them." replied Rean

Hemessean and Rean set away to greet their friends, it was so difficult to break free from all the other people around them, though they made their way through the crowds.

"Good day my friends, how was your night?" said   Hemessean to Jar and Saros

"We drank well and slept when the drink let us." Shouted back Jar

"Jar, you always drink so much, though why not, whatever makes you happy." Said Hemessean

"This is some hall, so massive, and so loud." Said Saros

"We should just stand here and wait for the call, and then I would imagine that things may go a little quieter?" said Rean

Rean and the others stud and waited for their call from the high council, they were told that many of the negative nasty's where forming, and that they would be informed on where they could be found. The high council was gathering together and everything was about to start, the long wooden tables of Casszoolas where filling and most of the high council was sitting waiting for the king of Casszoolas to arrive, once the king was there everything could start.

Many had come to see what could be done, as many was very worried and concerned about their welfare, the citizens of Casszoolas wanted to know who was going to rid them from this evil presence and how they would do such a task, they just needed to know everything would be done right and that them and their loved ones would be well.

The king entered the great hall the lighted hall was so full of people, it soon became quiet. As the great king found his seat, a shout from the guard master told everyone to stand in the names of Huzang the great king of Casszoolas.

The great council stud in a pledge of strength and unity and so did all the good people of Casszoolas, this was an important meeting where everyone who was anyone would be a part of the meeting and also the people of Casszoolas who wanted to see who was going to help them rid the negative nasty's,

The sun lighted shine found the kings face, as he sat and appreciated such a stance of loyalty from his faithful subjects, the great king looked at Ennin and said,

"Carry on Ennin, carry on."

Ennin the chief of all courts of the Casszoolas people called out,

"Our dear king Huzang of Casszoolas, guards, friends, and the good people we call you here today for one reason, to find a solution in the destruction of evil, in the name of the negative nasty's. we stand together today as a union of defiance against this evil, we shall no longer stand and watch the negative nasty's destroy any more of our good people, it is time to call for the end of   all   negative   nasty's."

After Ennin spoke to them, Ennin called out for Rean, Saros, Hemessean, and Jar,

"My good friends, we welcome you back to Casszoolas, and hope your stay with our good people is to your requirements, and you feel welcomed here in the arm of Casszoolas, you have been asked to attend such a large public meeting in the name of Huzang our great king, for a matter of the most urgency, we have asked for your help to rid the people of Casszoolas of the evil presence, the negative nasty, this evil has become a great threat on our wellbeing, so we ask you, hear today as the sun shines on our living skin, will you help the people of Casszoolas destroy the evil that is the negative nasty's?"

Rean stud and looked up towards the king and the great council of Casszoolas and said,

"we stand in front of all of you, with strength and goodness held deep within our hearts, the answer is and can only be…yes, we will rid you all of this evil that torments and threatens the good of humanity, we stand tall against this evil and will fight until our last breath if need be, I Rean, guardian of all light, and my protectors Jar, Saros and Hemessean, will serve the light towards all of your hearts and let it be known to all, on this day we swear to terminate this evil away for good, for the new day will rise and your children will play without the fear of the negative nasty, we shall rid you of this evil, to our last breath." Rean, Jar, Saros and Hemessean bowed to the king and the great council and then turned   and   bowed   to   the   people   of   Casszoolas.

The people of Casszoolas cheered out in happiness and overcome with gratitude, the applause lasted a good few minutes, with the applause also coming from the king and the great council, the hall was full of the sound of hope.

Hope that filled the room

That found a light

The song of human might

Strength in togetherness

They stand to the smile of life

O, love stands with them all

Within all their beating hearts

Forming the sound within hope

This new day is dancing

To the sound of our sun's smile

Let all colours find them

Find strength to rid thy evil

Seek the light towards this day

When birth made death cry

The people came together

This sun did shine

Towards new life being free

All abundance of air finds the free lungs

Find thy might

We shall, we shall

Show thy heart into sands of time

Humanity will rise true

For the light is always within us

Open thy eye's new born

See this wonder that is light

This beauty will be with us

Let thy in, let thy in

Show a friend thy heart

A hand from skin to skin

Love this lighted day

Show the dance its way

The Plan

This was no easy task, for the negative nasty's wear evil nasty slippery creatures, only the skilled could destroy such a monster of the world, Rean, Jar, Saros and Hemessean all knew what was in front of them and what was needed was a great plan, after the great hall meeting Rean, Jar, Saros and Hemessean were asked to attend a less formal meeting, though a very important meeting at that, a meeting of planning with Ennin the chief of all courts had a great plan and had a few people that could also help with the obliteration of the negative nasty's, Rean, Jar, Saros and Hemessean set away to one of the large rooms just away from the great hall and waited for Ennin to arrive.

Rean, Jar, Saros and Hemessean, walked into the room and sat at a large old wooden table, it was truly massive must have come from a great old tree, the room was covered in wooden slats with wonderful paintings from the great artist Galack, who was famous for his works of abstraction, a true wonder of painting. On the great wooden table lay drinks and bread and the strange fruit of Casszoolas, a taste of curiosity, a very strange taste, just in case anyone was feeling the need of something to eat while waiting for the others to arrive.

The   doors   opened,

"Welcome Rean, Jar, Saros and Hemessean, it is good to see you found the room, have you eaten?" said Ennin

"No…were too animated Ennin, were full of energy and eager to start, were so ready for this." Said Rean

"Good my friends let me introduce, Warham, leader of the lighted opals." Said Ennin

Rean looked at Warham and nodded,

"Good day my friend, it is an honour to sit with you, let us sit well and find heart within this sun lighted day and find a plan to whorl this evil into its own darkness."

Warham looked directly at Rean and said,

"Rean, Jar, Saros and Hemessean, my friends, yes we shall overcome this evil that casts over our beloved Casszoolas, I was asked to attend this meeting by our good friend Ennin, I have many good loyal troops of the lighted opals, to serve against this evil, we have trained in the use of power of light against the negative nasty's, for years we have worked and many are ready."

"This brings warmth to our hearts Warham, we welcome you and you good troops of the light to join our fight against this darkness, yes, your most welcome," replied Rean

"Let us all sit and find a way to rid this evil, come friend's gathered with me and see this." Said Ennin

Ennin showed Warham, Rean, Jar, Saros and Hemessean a long old book she had taken from the old library of Casszoolas courts, it had listed of a case of many years ago, of such a man called Jennet, who found a way of sealing the negative within and using the energies to direct back the negative to positive.

"Look this was from a long time ago?" said Warham

Rean looked at Ennin and winked and smiled, Warham looked back at Ennin, and said,

"Have I missed something?"

"No my friend, Rean, Jar, Saros and Hemessean could easily go back in time and find this Jennet." Said Ennin

"Yes, I forgot we have the warriors of the light with us, Yes...*that's* wonderful, I didn't think." Said Warham

"You would need to get Jennet to show you how it could be achieved, "said Ennin

Rean looked to Ennin and said,

"Yes, it can be done, though it would take me a day to find my lighted energies, you see I have to think and find the one within, it was shown to me by the Great Aldus."

"That will be fine, while you're preparing yourself we shall work on the training more, for it shall be a difficult task." Said Ennin "yes, though, we must keep this information just with our hearts for now no one should know what we are planning, it must only be with us, is this understood my friends." Called out Rean

Everyone looked at Rean and answered back,

"Yes Rean, within our hearts, within our hearts only!"

"Hemessean I will need your help, Jar, Saros you go with Warham and help them with the training, go now my friends and let the light be with you, we shall find you in a few days."

Said Rean

"We shall do as you wish friend, we shall go with Warham and show him the ways of the light, and we shall learn from them also, for now Rean and Hemessean it is goodbye, we hope all goes well and you find Jennet, goodbye." Said Jar

"Come Hemessean; let us go now we have much to do." Said Rean

Rean and Hemessean said farewell to Ennin and walked towards the temple of Casszoolas, a place of thoughtfulness where Rean could find the light within and travel through time, through the ever changing air, within everything passed and new to find Jennet, to learn the secret of using the negative and using it for the positive, if Rean could find this then this gift would be of great use against the all evil negative nasty's. he knew that to find his light within would be a difficult task, and he was also looking forward to showing Hemessean, his true love, the ways of the light, Rean knew that their love was strong and that would also be a great help against the fight of evil, though he also knew that being with Hemessean was one of the most wonderful experiences he held with him always, when things became tough… the feeling that someone was with him was a wonderful strength to hold, Rean wanted to show Hemessean his true light and become one with her. To share such a thing was beyond most living beings, most people come together through their orgasm, the principal of togetherness, the human bond, when we reach our orgasm we are close to the light that takes us when we pass into the air, though the orgasm shows life its new light and two become to new start, our new born find use through the light within the love of two become all new. Rean knew that coming together within the light is the most wonderful bond any living being could do, and this could easily happen while he finds his light to travel, in doing such a delightful thing will show Hemessean Rean's true love for her, and Hemessean will experience her light within, true love and pleasure of body and mind, the wonder of the philosophy towards everything, within our being, the consommé of life where our new born are waiting and the dead are becoming everything new a truly magnificent place. This could only be found through his complete devotion to the light within everything good, the all power that he finds deep within his heart, this power does not need for pain, this food to his love shall not cry, for today his light will shine within and find his everything. To become the light Rean needed to find meditation through self being, and waiting for Hemessean to

135

follow, this would be how they could connect while traveling through the air to find Jennet.

Rean and Hemessean walked to a tall white tower with just one door and the windows where on the top of the tower to let in all the light, this was a place to find one's self and meditate, an ideal place for Rean and Hemessean to start their journey within time and light.

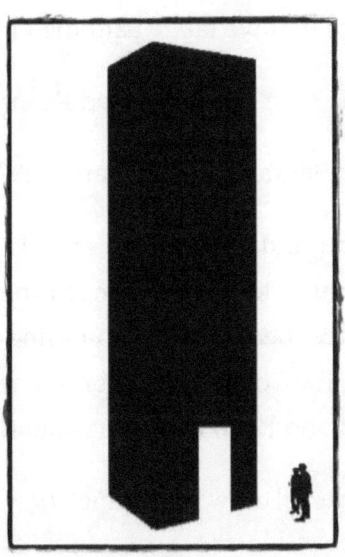

Within time this journey will find

With all surroundings the light found Rean and Hemessean, they walked into the tower of light and found just one being standing waiting for them,

"Welcome my friends." He said

"Good day, good day friend." Replied Rean and Hemessean

"I am here just for a while to show you around and welcome you, I will secure the doors and protect the tower until your both finished and ready to come out, I understand that it is in complete confidence that we talk." Said the kind man

"Thank you, what is your name?" asked Rean

"My name is Luhan, let me show you around." He said

Luhan showed Rean and Hemessean around the tower, though there wasn't that much to show them, in the middle of the tall tower was a square bed and surrounding the bed was tall candle's all alight, the room was adorned with brilliant white, they looked around and Rean turned to Luhan and said,

"Yes…this is wonderful now it is time for you to leave us my friend."

"Yes, yes Rean as you wish, I wish you both a safe journey." Replied   Luhan

Luhan turned and walked out toward the large doors, he walked outside and closed them and stud guard waiting for Rean and Hemessean.

Rean and Hemessean walked towards the large bed in the centre of the tower Rean looked into Hemessean's eyes and said,

"My Hemessean… my love, my light, on this day let me show you my true self, my love for you."

Hemessean smiled at Rean and said,

"I am willing to do anything you wish my love, show me the way." Kissing Rean's neck

Rean and Hemessean started to kiss taking off each other's clothes, standing naked kissing Rean stroked Hemessean's back, pulling her closer, Hemessean's breasts rubbing on Rean's chest, they fell onto the bed, first Hemessean then Rean the light from the tower caressing their naked body's making passionate love, Rean was deep inside of Hemessean, while Hemessean sat on Rean, Rean becoming more aroused, he whispered in Hemessean's ear,

"My love do you feel my love, do you feel me," he said as he pushed deeper into Hemessean

"Yes…yes my love, Rean I feel wonderful

Hemessean held tight to Rean as she shivered it wasn't long before they both lifted into orgasm, both in a sensual lock their body's became so tight to each other, Rean brought his head closer to Hemessean's and touched her forehead with his, saying,

"Now we can flow, I will show you my true love, become the light,"

As Rean's forehead touched Hemessean's a light found them, a wonderful light that released them from their physical body's, pitching them into the air, now free of their flesh, though their body's where completely safe, suspended in time, Rean and Hemessean now within the air travelling through light and air.

Time

Light

Air

We

Are

You

Are

Time

Deep within everything, together this dance with the everything, this is what only could be, through time shifting memories bliss,

Shifting

Towards

Everything

New

And

Old

Find them safe

Now travelling so fast though time and air, the very thing that everything is made from,

Everything

New

Within this

Everything

Show

Them

This

Wonderful

Everything

140

Everything

They fell through the wonders or time and air, now in thought could they communicate, though through their true love of each other they were completely safe within this soup of energies, this fantastic, this dance within all seeing light.

Rean   called   to   Hemessean,

"Oh…my love, see me now, see all around us, dance with me in this wonder, my love is all around you, I feel you everywhere, were so together hear, do you see?"

Hemessean called back to Rean,

"This is amazing, truly astonishing, were in our dance, this love is so true the magic of life everywhere all around us, I love you, I love you, with everything, I love you."

They fell deeper within the energy's, deeper and deeper, until they could feel a vibration, this was the time line, where they needed to join and find the right place in time to find jennet, they connected within the timeline, pushing them into a strange elevator, could have been described as a tall glass elevator with many openings, Rean called out to Hemessean and said,

When you see an opening that is lighted that is the one we need to find an travel through, once we travel through the opening we will become our physical self again, though it won't be our real physical self, just our dream self, do you understand?"

"Yes, Rean, I do understand, how does the opening know?" said Hemessean

"The opening connects with our memories and finds its reasoning and comes up with the correct opening and guides us to where we need to be."

"That is truly amazing." Shouted Hemessean

Rean and Hemessean passed through the lighted opening sending them into a small low lighted street, once they pull each other together they went to find Jennet, they knew where to find the inventor of the strange, Jennet's work had been well documented so there was plenty of books with most of the inventors work in.

"This looks like the place, let's go and see if we can find the inventor." Said Rean

With a very strange noise coming from an old barn like building Rean shouted out,

"Hello, hello is that Jennet?"

The noise stops…then the door opens and out walks the inventor, covered in oil and dust,

"Who's that, how do you know of my name?"

"Good day to you, my name is Rean and my friends name is Hemessean, we come from your future we need your help." Shouted Rean

Rean figured that just to come out with it straight-out would be more useful for the inventers head; he knew the way Jennet thinks after reading all the books about the inventor.

Jennet looked at them and said,

"Well…   you'd   better   come   in   then."

And walked inside the strange looking barn, Rean and Hemessean followed Jennet back into the barn, where their eyes were met with astonishment, it was like looking into an old museum, full of gadgets, steam machines, and clockwork dolls working on other strange machines, Rean thought it better not to ask what the hell the inventor was doing as he had read somewhere how the inventor didn't like to talk that much about his work.

"So...why me?" the inventor asked

"We need your help with the fight against the negative nasty's, their threating the people of your future and you know something that we need to know." Replied Rean

"ha, the negative nasty's, a hideous thing, I know what you need to know, let me go find my notes on the positive from negative, I won't be long, please wait here for a short while." Said Jennet

The inventor walked up an old staircase each step blowing out a spin of dust, while muttering,

"Where did I put that note book, where o where is it, ah, that's the one."

the inventor soon came back with an old dusty book full of bits of paper falling out, he walk back to Rean and Hemessean, flinging the book next to them on a table close by, knocking over a few bottles of strange looking liquid, Rean wasn't going to ask what was   in   the   bottles.

"This is what you need, I suppose you will need to read it all, or may be page four to twenty-seven, that should do it, yes, just that part will be all you need, I'll be around if you need me, though I must get back to work." Said the inventor

Rean sat with Hemessean and studded everything the inventor wrote.

"So the negative can be dislodged, like it is just a thought processed in the brain, everything is connected...I knew this though until reading this it didn't make sense, though now I see, I see how it can be done, we really can do this." Said Rean to himself

Rean and Hemessean thanked the inventor and gave him his note book back, they set off back to the opening, and travelled back from the time line into the energy soup, now flowing again with each other, Rean said to Hemessean,

"we have to let everything go, become the air around us, just feel everything around you and flow within, this will send us back to our being, our flesh, our living body's, don't worry… nothing can harm you, I won't let it trust me." Said Rean

They fell within the air everything holding them, placing their light back within the physical plane, becoming hole and with the beating of hearts, they awaken laying naked holding each other, Rean kissed Hemessean and said,

"I   Love   you."

"And I do you." Replied Hemessean

They lay within the light, the light restoring their energy's like new, Rean and Hemessean touched the door way and it open with Luhan standing smiling,

"Welcome my friends."

"Did you get what you went for?" asked Luhan

"Yes, we did, we now have just what we need, and we should go straight away and see Ennin and see what we should do next." Replied Rean

They set away back to the great hall to speak to Ennin, Rean now had everything he needed, he was ready to start the journey and find the negative nasty's, all he wanted was to rid Casszoolas of this evil, for good, he was so sick of their menace, they had to be destroyed for the good of all the people, had to destroy them.

Within the great hall Ennin was waiting for Rean and Hemessean to arrive, Ennin was keen to hear what was talked about, while Rean and Hemessean where away there had been another attack on someone from Casszoolas by the negative nasty, the poor man was left for dead, they controlled his mind until they had what they needed, the poor man Wallis worked for the courts, they got into his head and found loads of information on the high court's plans on what they were planning to do to the negative nasty's.

Wallis did not know what he was doing so it was not his fault, it was the evil that had over taken his mind and body, though they now have a lot of very important information, after leaving him for dead, that poor man is now fighting for his life, they expect he won't make tomorrow, all that is left of him is a sick body, a lost soul, so confused, and not knowing where he is, you see when the negative nasty's are done with you they don't just leave the body, they take everything, so that the host cannot give any useful information when they come around, nothing, their just a shell of confused flesh, a saddened shell of the once magnificent self.

Towards the darkness he lay within nothing but his dismay, nothing has he left, no wanting no nothing, just a stare an empty Stare poor thing, they have taken his memories his everything, a shell of bone and skin poor thing, look out and see the darkened gaze, looking deep into the big blackened eyes like tunnels, never ending tunnels of the darkest deep poor thing, to think of what he was, so strong and bright, so tall with might, nothing could have foreseen such a thing, a true act of darkness did fall upon him poor thing, poor thing.

It won't be long before he's gone his body will rot into the dusted space, the space within the empty nothing, and once such a light so bright. They must destroy that negative nasty before more fall this way, it's such an evil death leaving nothing within, stop them and do it fast or soon everything we become the past, the blue skies will become so grey, our children will never play, the air will become dark and thick choking our lungs crushing the breathing into dusted gags, no air, no air, falling to the ground, so fast so weak, they must be stop at every cost, this evil surging through the living distorting the truth when over taking everything new telling lies and taking over, only to leave with such a waist leave the body confuse and with haste.

Take warning stands such darkness in your living world, just like in this story you read today, a negative nasty lives close to you, telling you of friendship while they drain you, the darkest of rain clouds will follow you around eating away the goodness from your heart, leaving nothing when ready to go, so be warned and look around, don't end up like poor Wallis poor thing, poor thing.

It was deep into the night before Rean and Hemessean arrived at the great hall, they were really upset to hear such sad news that there had been a new attack; they went straight to see Ennin, to see if anything could be done for poor Wallis, though clearly nothing could be done for the poor man. Rean and Hemessean walked into the great hall greeted by Ennin,

"Welcome back Rean and Hemessean, welcome; it's wonderful to see you both, may I say... you both look wonderful,"

Rean and Hemessean smiled back at Ennin,

"Why thank you Ennin, it was an amazing journey, we found what we went for; it was truly astonishing to feel so free." Said Rean

"Tell me…any news on Wallis? Such sad news met us about the negative nasty, we feel for him, any news Ennin?" asked Rean

"He's not doing very well, he doesn't have long to go, it is so sad to see him in this way, Wallis was a true friend and I shall miss him greatly, we are losing too many friends of late, and the negative nasty's are becoming stronger by the day." Replied Ennin

"We should go see him straight away!" said Hemessean

"Yes I will take you now, come with me." Replied Ennin

They walked towards the hospital wing of Casszoolas, a long dark passage where the sick and heeling where been looked after, somewhere ok to be with others, though some like Wallis where too sick and too distressing to see of the others, so they had to be in separate rooms, they got closer to the ward where Wallis was been looked after, a brighter corridor, with four doors one of the had Wallis's name wrote on, on a sheet of paper. They walked into the room.

The bed was empty; Wallis was in the corner of the room crying, he was muttering "where am I?"…"please help me, who am I?"

It was so very sad to see him this way, they all remember seeing him at the great meeting a few days ago and now he's so lost, they looked at him with tears falling from their eyes, Rean kneels down to Wallis, he puts his hand on Wallis's arm and gently says,

"Oh…my friend, do not worry so, we are your friends, we cannot hurt you, we are here for you, listen can you hear me?"

Wallis just stares through Rean's eyes; he's lost so lost nothing could help him, now, nothing.

"Do not worry my friend all will be well, do not cry, all will be well." Said Rean

That was all Rean could say he and the others knew that it wouldn't be long before he died, and they wanted to be quick so that he could not suffer any more than he already had done. This was true evil at its very worst.

Rean looked at Hemessean and Ennin and said,

"We should help Wallis back into his bed."

"Yes, we will." They replied

They pick him up and put him to bed, gently stroking his forehead, and siting with him until a few hours later Wallis died, he was with friends and went fast.

His lifeless body lay deep into the cotton sheets, Rean, Hemessean and Ennin's heads bowed Rean whispers,

"We shall get them for you my friend, we shall find them."

The darkened hail, from the end of time showing life its true evil, to find the evil that took dear Wallis away, Rean and the other have a tall tail do reach for the darkness will find them all, they should stand together...stand tall one and all. This evil that is coming to say hello has taken many and live within the unfortunate unknowing friends, deep within the living they wait within for time will tell how this evil will dwell upon their unknowing pray, stand tall Rean, show the darkness its true light, save everything new for our tomorrow day is not that far away, they need this man to show them his way, the way of light within the fight, so when the darkened retch comes knocking on their door light will shine through and show evil its way and it shall decree on more.

They stand with open arms, the unknowing what will be found, on this day when darkness fall, what will happen to one and all.

Light of sovereign

Shine from our sky

Show the evil

On its way

Send it far away

From old into new

With willing and strength

They stand tall to the evil

Hand in hand

With beating heart stand thy strong

Wisdom know all so true

Within this tale lives' you

Our beautiful light sing true, sing new

Everything that Rean and the others had trained for, to protect the light from the evil was soon to be tested, they were in for a fight that only the strongest could win, this darkness was at its very most.

Rean had noticed a darkness falling within the sky's he wondered what would become of everything, through all his training and studying Rean always new that one day it would all come true. All Rean had to do was to remain on a positive plane, and stay true within his mind.

The powers of positive thinking can sing true, once put in its place nothing can touch it, it's the strongest weapon against any darkened menace, this strength is inside everyone and Rean new that was what he was going to do show the people of Casszoolas the way of the light, it was the only way to stop the dark from coming in.

Set to my friend

Stand to thy light

Hold thy strength within you

Once it is in place

It shall never leave you

An essential tool of life

That can only be placed by a friend

This lighted positivity

Will shine within you

All that is needed

Is the light

The light within you

Wallis was laid to rest, many where feeling uneasy with all the deaths and the uncertainty of who would be next. Rean and the others had to work fast to find their way through this darkened time, Ennin called out to Rean and the others for everyone to meet back at the great hall of Casszoolas.

It was late at night before everyone arrived the feeling where strong, many with frustrations and it was written all over their faces, they had to act fast and the only way was for everyone to come together. The great hall was full; it was late at night and most where tired though it was at the utmost importance that the meeting would start strait away so the Rean and the others could act.

Within the great hall stud Rean, Hemessean, Jar, Saros and Warham the leader of the lighted opals, also in the great hall stud Ennin the great chief of all courts, and all of the great council and the King of Casszoolas, King Huzang was the first to talk, everything was ready for them to stand up a plan, this darkness could not be allowed to stay within the good people of Casszoolas.

With everyone in the great hall king Huzang addressed Rean, Hemessean, Jar, Saros and Warham, and Ennin,

"Welcome my good friends, protectors of light, on this day it saddens my heart when I talk of such evil among this wonderful dwelling we live in, I cannot remember such a darkened time of our history that has overtaken our living and no longer can we stand for any more of this sickness to fall upon our good people, so with that I ask you my friends, it is time...it is time to rise above this darkness and once again see the light."

154

The great king looked up into the great windows of the great hall and said,

"See the light that shines within the eye of our friends their children playing, dancing within the sound of everything new, yes...it is time for our wonder, I say now go darkness, go away, from my people...I see not your reasoning, you dwell within such evil, be gone from our hearts, and never to be returned, we stand tall against your evil ways...we shall overcome your misery and lay you to sleep forever into the misty darkened hallow where you belong, without rest we shall hunt you, with speed to your demise and you should listen when we say go now, know thy voice feel my light through your darkened mass we shall live, life within this light seeing off your evil ways, be gone...be gone."

Rean, Hemessean, Jar, Saros and Warham, and Ennin, stud and applauded the king,

"The words spoken from a true king" Said Ennin standing and applauding the king,

The king sat into his seat and Ennin spoke,

"What word do you bring from time and space Rean, please tell us, do you think it is feasible to think that we could actually overcome this evil that scorns our way of living, tell us what news?"

Rean   stud   to   the   court   and   said,

"On this day it shall be known that yes…we can do this, think of a mathematical calculation that you thought could not be reasoned, though if you sit down and really look at the way the numbers sit together, soon you will see how it all flows, like what is all around us every day every second, the running of water becoming the shape of everything it sits in, the water is showing it spectator a lesson, when we drink can it not become in the shape of the glass? When we drink the water…can it not become the shape of your throat, and while sitting inside our stomach can it not become the shape of your stomach? The answer is yes! And, this lessen is to overcome the darkness, this evil noose hanging over our necks, we shall become within the shape of this darkness."

A gasp finds the hall

"no, no…do not worry – yes we have to take shape, though not through our way of the use of light, you see…everything around us is created to generate new life, the light feeding everything, growing, nourishing our world. Also our light shows us the same way the water can, in that within our light we also the dark…that is our shadow."

Rean passed and looked at everyone and then said,

"Our answer is simply we fight the darkness, with our darkness, our shadows, yes… it sounds insane, though when I went to see Jennet, I read in the inventors notes that apart of us live within our   shadows.

"And how do we become our shadows?" asked Ennin

"Within our light hold strong reflections that give out messages, like when we talk sound travels through the air and light, in the same way parts of our being also travels through the light, Jennet called it the reflective inner self, this is the transition from body into dark matter showing our self through shadow, the shadow is waiting for us all the time, we take many things around us for granted, if only we spent more time appreciating everything around us and really started to see then life would be so much easier…you often here of people say the same thing just after a near death experience, they start to appreciate the small things again and really look at life. Jennet wrote this in his notes, it is very exciting when it all clicks in your head, negative into positivity." Replied Rean

Rean looked up at everyone; he raised his hand and said,

"Look at the hand then look to the ground, look at the shadow, and keep looking just at the shadow."

Everyone gazed intensely at Rean's shadow on the floor of the great hall, next to Rean's actual body stud a set of large candles alighted as it was very late at night, Rean then closed his eyes and pronounced to his shadow,

"as I stand hear within this massive hall I see you, as before your ever presence with me standing towards the lighted twitch from the flame dancing within this scented wind, though this time my shadow I see you, and I say to you as I do when I move,

157

when I breathe, Oh, shadow, put out that lighted candle, put it out."

Rean pointed at one of the flickering candles standing upright alongside all the others in the great hall, and once again said,

"Put it out...out the light."

Rean's shadow started to move towards the dancing flickering flame, somehow the shadow leaped away from the darkened home, and found the flame, taking the flame away into the darkness, leaving nothing but a smoking candle, standing cold next to the others still dancing and flickering in flame.

"He did it...he really did it?"

"Oh, that's amazing!"

"That's unreal, how did he do that?"

Shouts of amazement found and echoed around the great hall while Rean whispered,

"Thank you my shadow, and welcome, we see each other at last, your me and I you, I thank you."

Rean turned to everyone and said,

"The power of the knowing, expressive is the light that finds us, when we raise from new born we have so many tools within ourselves, though how can we know them without lesson, show thy self the everything within and thy will grow to see, to become self-aware and hold everything around us, so you see it is with us and can be done."

Rean passed to the council and said

"we can do this, the evil is strong, and knows many way of manipulating our minds, though we also can be as strong and get into the darkness, though it has never been achieved before and could be very dangerous, as we do not know what will happen, and once within the darkness…the probabilities of climbing out of the revolting scorn would be very small, though we have to do this, the heart of the darkness is the only way to face this evil…we have to do this and soon."

"What will it take Rean, what will we do?" asked Ennin

Rean hung his head; his shoulder hung deep down, and then like a bright light with a jump he replied,

"Our plan will start now, we have no time to waist, so listen all, to travel into the heart of this evil we need to find the new negative nasty…yes, the negative nasty are nothing compared to the new threat, I have been told from my good old friend Hassam that from the dead tree new evil intensifications arises and they are known as **cutters** a genetic made from the pure sickness from the suffering of our kinds, all of the screams taken from the dyeing before the negative nasty leaves the body they take the screams and put them into the dead tree, where the cutter has been growing, that is the new evil that we need to find and need to   enter."

A strange silence found the great hall, and then Ennin said

"And how could this be achieved Rean?" Ennin had a tear falling from her eye

Rean looked straight at Ennin and said,

"The only way...the only hope we have is to travel back to the dead tree and try and find where the cutter is, it will be very dangerous and some will fall within the darkest of holes never to return, though we have no other choice, we have to go find the cutter before they find us, because if they find us when were not ready that would be the end of all, so listen to me and I shall say this, I shall walk into the darkness, and I shall place the brightest of glows within it darkened heart, they will be hope in this hall tonight, I call to all and say, when you close your eyes tonight sleep well for tomorrow we go into the darkest of our journeys so far."

Rean looked at Warham and said

"Stand tall your lighted opals, make them knowing of their task, and follow me into the dark as we hunt down this evil."

Warham bowed to the King and then to Rean and said,

"It is with haste I go into the night and stand to my own, we shall be ready for you when you see fit Rean"

Warham walked into the night towards his troops knowing he had much to do. Rean then called to the council,

160

"while we are gone we shall hold a light over Casszoolas, this will protect you all, if we succeed the light will stay strong, if I am to fail the light will fall, though we should not think of that, I know I will succeed and overcome this troubled time."

The council said fair well to Rean, and the king went his way to secure everything would be in place within Casszoolas.

Rean turned to Hemessean, Jar and Saros and said,

"Well my friends, it will soon be time to do what we have trained for, so stand well and tomorrow we shall go deep into the darkest of all hallows, I have been before and have never forgotten the screaming from the walking ghosts, the dead trees are truly evil, we must remember the light, be positive in all situations, and we will overcome all the darkness that is ahead of us."

Jar looked at Rean and said,

"We are concerned about you, Rean…we don't want you to die like the others that have been in such close contact with this evil."

Rean smile back at Jar and replied,

"I understand your troubles, though now I am so very strong and I know more than I ever did and could have wished for, so my friends, do not let doubt find your mind, do not listen to the darkness that plays tricks with you wonder, listen to my heart beat, I give you my light find thy dancing towards all new life, come celebrate with me my friends, for tomorrow we shall start our journey fresh and new, no need for the doubt…send that away with the flame that my shadow put out...yes, send your doubt within that."

"Oh, Rean, you hold so much for your friends, we feel everything you just spoken and it shall hold us strong, for tomorrow we shall follow our friend into the darkest of holes, though we shall not worry, we shall instead be tall and walk strong with no doubt, we know he will overcome this evil that has risen over our heads, we know that all shall be bright again and the people of Casszoolas." Replied Jar with a smile

Rean looked back at his good friends and said,

Listen to thy self

Open minded

Self all around

Do thy friend with light

Adorn this truth

Seeing through the new

For this light one

Will stand true

Never forget

Stand with truth within

Be positive within

Let thy children see

Into the ever new they come

And we must

We must show the dark our strength

Our love within

Shall dance within this day

Hold strong where we went so wrong

And see everything around us

Take shape

Like our water ways

And use the way

For our next day

We the seekers of all good

Will follow another

Into the dark

For unity

Shall shine through

163

Now show thy way

My people on this day

Through the light we shall travel

And seek the truth

Overcome all evil

Standing within this forest of the malevolent

We shall never fall to their way

Only to stand tall

And come through of the next

Our next sun lighted day

"Friends, I will not lie to you it will be a difficult time for us all, though if we stay strong we can do anything, don't have doubt in thy mind, instead hold tall every part of light and goodness you could ever hold, for a positive thing can be an added strength towards the battle of evil we have in front of us all." Said Rean

Jar and Saros turned and walked out of the great hall leaving Hemessean and Rean, Hemessean looked deep into Rean's eyes and   said,

"I believe Rean, everything you have shown me so far has been for the good of the light and I have fallen deeply in love with you and everything you stand for, so when I say I will follow you I say it with my heart, Oh, Rean...with my heart I hold you and hope that we overcome our fight, for when we are done I want to live with you and become one again, it was so amazing, you're the light that opens my eyes."

Rean smiled and held Hemessean in a tight embrace whispering in her ear,

"My love, we shall overcome these days of darkness and soon it shall shine again with abundance of light falling on our children's faces, light will overcome everything.

In dream we find within the storyline

Dancing ghosts within our dreams

Chapter Nine

Into The Woods

Rean was handed some notes found long ago by an old traveller, he read them out to the others before they entered the old dark wood.

Into the woods the path of darkness they follow, this darkened hollow, only with bravery and light they stand and fight the evil retch.

Looking out for the Cutter with the darkest of night, follow them with all its spite, this monster of the worst crawling and sniffing the unrespecting out, just for the death a trophy to hail a glimpse of the certainly not never, a twitch to the neck then down you go with nothing inside but a massive hole.

When darkness surrounds you with all it's might look out for the cutter, it wants to take you where no one will find you that horrid from all darkness will leave you for dead.

So listen out when all light is out, keep calm if you hear a shout, that won't be the cutter he's ever so meddlesome though a want to take away everything good, and that's what he normally is, they will have to be strong, make shore nothing goes wrong, keep their ears to the ground, for the cutter is all around, don't shuffle he will hear you, don't move he can see you through the darkened trees.

When in the dark woods remember don't touch the trees, their dead rotting flesh will take your skin and leave you a walking ghost, listen good and listen true for everything the light tells you, or you won't last too long, everything will fall long gone, if you stay with your friends then they won't find you until the end, stay close and open your eyes if you hear a whimper don't be surprised, many have fallen into the dead tree's with their flesh taken away and becoming the tree, walking forever with nothing to do, but cry and cry, don't let that happen to you, stand close to all and one, listen to everything that going on, don't forget never touch the trees, and keep listening walk slowly with your feet.

Listen to these words and you journey should go with ease; don't forget it and you will find your way.

Stand strong within your hearts, don't let doubt burden your friendship, let in the light from all you see, stand tall with one and all, you shall find it new and everything around you, listen deep and look twice, for what is can sometime be strange to the eye, remember to tell a time when long since gone within these words where ever so strong, the darkened haze that finds your way will remember everything you do and tell-tale the cutter and show him the way. When you breathe make it short don't talk too loud for they will hear you and seek you out. All ways listen to everything told, wisdom from their words should be held deep within your soul, never forgotten. Soon you will be making your first steps within the wood, things are wonderfully good, they shine like diamonds and taste of spice, a taste you will have never tasted before and will want you coming back for more, don't be greedy, have one or two and let that be that, or you'll get stuck in the wonderfully good and become so fat, listen up and listen good. These words come from the heart and stay within the ink on this paper old, the words come new to you and so they should do.

The dark woods are full of evil mischief so be warned don't be fooled into thinking what is seen is always the truth, look deep with everything new, take nothing for granted, lookout for the sculpture of the bees, the bees will find you, sting you and poison your mind, this leaves you within a hypnotic daze, so the cutter can find you and have his way.

The sculpture of the bees

There isn't much more to be told so when your finished reading these notes try and remember to take it all in, they will help you from getting into a meddlesome spin. When you're done fold them up and send them back so these words can talk again, and one more thing, be well on your journey through the darkened woods.

Rean carefully folded up the old notes and gave them back to the old traveller,

"Thank you they have truth within them and I remember the dead trees, a very nasty place, so I know there is some truth with these notes, we thank you sir."

The old traveller nodded his head and said,

"Good day too you all and I wish you all well, goodbye." And with that he walked away and disappeared.

Everyone was standing back in the front of the woods, very nervous and very hesitant.

Into the twisting darkness they walked with some unknowing, the darkness was immense a truly foreboding wrench to the heart that knocked on all of them all, leaving everyone standing in the massive of horrid feeling ever so small.

They split up as the forest was ever so enormous over towering everyone, Warham set off with the lighted opals, and Rean, Hemessean, Jar and Saros set away to a other direction, they thought it be better and be easier to cover more ground. They all set away with haste.

Deep into the woods they went, they could only just see the next tree in front of them; they knew it was going to be difficult. The only way was strait through the old wood, where maybe the finding of the cutter would end all the death and misery.

They walked close together, almost shoulder to shoulder, they didn't know what to expect no one had really seen the cutter, all that was known was the cutter ruled the negative nasty's, so they had to be very cautious in the woods, anything could happen so they walked slowly.

"This muddy ground is very difficult to walk in, the mud is getting everywhere." Said Jar

"Yes, the woods are full of this unforgiving dirt, though I remember that when we get within the middle of the wood the dirt becomes less wet, and much easier to walk through, it won't be long my friends, let us keep on, this way." Replied Rean

A strange chilling sound came from the trees,

"What was that?" said Hemessean

"Just try and keep walking, we can't stop for anything; time is going so fast and where so far from where we need to be." Said Rean

Again the chilling sound echoed towards the four, within the darkened chill became a figure walking towards Rean and the others, Rean looked up, he stepped forward engaging the figure approaching them and said,

"Hello, who is this that approaches?"

No voice replied

Closer and closer the figure came,

"Is   it   the   cutter?"   said   Jar

"Stand in line and get ready, I shall make the first move then you all follow, though let me talk first, it may not be the cutter." Said Rean

"Where looking for the cutter, we mean you no harm, just tell us who you are and we shall let you on your way." Said Rean to the approaching figure

It soon became apparent that the approaching figure was just an old traveller going his way through the old woods; Rean asked the old traveller if he knew of the cutter,

"hello, we are four young people like your self's looking for the cutter, that is not something I would want to run into, I have seen the cutter from a long distance, and that's as far as I would ever want to be near the cutter, such evil I have never seen before that day, let me tell you all, be prepared." Said the old traveller

"Tell me traveller, we need to know what does the cutter look like and where can we find it?" Shouted out Rean

"The cutter is tall, very tall, and you'll see it from a long way away and also the smell…it's the most disgusting smell I have ever sniffed, horrid truly the worst smell!, if you want my advice I would stay well away from it…the cutter was dragging ropes behind it attached where bodies many hanging and dangling, some dragging in the mud, the stench is disgusting, I was a good mile or two away and it made me sick." Replied the old traveller

The old traveller was doing a few drawings in the woods, he often come to the woods to draw, on that day the old traveller found the cutter and did this drawing of it, and this is the only drawing of the cutter.

The Cutter

Rean and the others looked at each other with dread within their eye, such evil,

"What was the cutter doing with all the dead?" asked Rean

"why sir, the cutter was taking them to the warren, the warren is where the cutter lives, you can find the warren deep within the middle of the circle of dead trees, be warned just standing within the middle of the circle of the dead trees is enough to kill most people, soon as you step into the circle the hex of the warren will find its victim, such evil, such an evil foreboding part of this world, stay way!" shouted the old traveller

"Now I have to be on my way, I wish you all well; if you follow my old footsteps through the mud they will take you where I last watched the cutter, good day."

The old traveller lifted up his timeworn hat and walked away from them muttering to himself, "they should just turn back, their too young to die, far too young."

Rean, Hemessean, Saros, and Jar followed the old traveller's foot mud prints; deeper and deeper they walked into the darkness, the twisting branches weaving a maze of uncertainty towards the warren, the place of the cutter.

"Listen friends, when we find the warren, let me enter the middle, the hex will not harm me, I am protected, you three would be in danger, so it will be up to me, when I enter it will be up to you three to make shore no one enters, this will give me more of a chance to find the cutter." Said Rean

They walked for miles into the deepest of darkness, surrounded by hallowed screams, and the stench over whelming, the stench of rotting flesh, the stench of death. The old travellers foot prints where becoming harder to find as the wood was becoming dryer as they got closer to the centre of the wood, water would not go to the centre of the wood, this made the four very uneasy, as they remembered what Rean had said about the water taking shape where ever it went and for water not to go to place only meant it was an evil place.

"Stay close, I feel something, where nearly there, keep quiet, not a sound, everyone put your masks on so you can't smell the stench, it will only make you vomit, stay close." Said Rean

An uneasy feeling found them , an overwhelming sadness hovered within their being, feeling like the darkest of day was upon them, only the strongest of hearts could overcome this darkened retch, the saddens the misery, playing with all their minds, casting the very worst of grey eyed monsters among the four brave protectors. They always remembered what Rean told them to keep the light within their hearts and that would see away any kind of sadness, so they dug deep within their hearts.

A shine found them; this rising shine overcame the depression and formed a protective globe around them, so that if any other mischief wondered by they would be ready for such a thing.

"So you see the truth of the light within really can work, and with all you love and light combined the darkness is not as strong, keep it with you we are nearly there, I can feel it, it's very strong, this won't be easy, though we must take shape of the light we must fly within the darkness and hold our light within showing this evil the light, we can do this, we can do anything as long as we hold the light within our hearts.

Towards

Into the dark

Forwards

So they march

With light

To change the dark

Defending the truth

With the heart

Only they will see

With truth and courageousness they walk into the evil, the circle of the dead trees, the most foreboding of revolting dwellings, a dark hole of evil, twisting in the pain from tortured scream, where only the suffering would be seen, trees of human flesh standing in a circle of misery and pain, while their empty souls are left to wonder in a tormented chain, in the middle stud a tall dark hold built of blooded cold greyed stone weaved with bones and flesh, the warren the cutters hole, where the dammed could live free from light, to exist of the tormented tortured might. The cutters hole standing tall, in stench, in rotting mess finds Rean and the others, standing with light that will see them into this hell to save the light of the people of Casszoolas.

This circle so full of pain it must have taken so many good people to feed such insanity, they stud and gazed around in hesitation though knowing the light will always win.

Standing tall

The only way was inwards towards the darkness and nothing could be done, this was the time, everything counted on it, Rean and the other new that if they could find the cutter they had a chance to stop this evil, they was glad to have seen the old traveller and very happy that he did the drawing of the cutter, at least they had an idea of what they were looking for, this hideous monster of the dark dead forest was not going to get away.

They walked deep within the circle of dead trees, Rean warned everyone never to touch the trees, the only way to destroy such an evil monster was to find the cutter and let him try and take over one's being, it was scary that the very fact of losing to the cutter and never remembering one's self, one's friends, and most of all Rean would lose his memories of his love for Hemessean. This was very distressing Rean knew he had only one chance to get into the cutters inner self, even the evil cutter had that weakness, everything that was living deep down had some kind of a being, Rean had studied in great detail about jumping into evil minds and overtaking them, though he also had read of one that tried a similar execution on an evil presence and didn't make it, he was trapped with the evil and left with nothing but his wandering ghost. Rean was determined never to fall like that his plan was intensive, Rean had told Jar, Saros, and Hemessean, that when he entered the cutter under no circumstances should they try to get him out, Rean knew that the only way out was by destroying the cutter, if they tried to get Rean out before he was ready,   the   cutter and Rean would become one, that would not be good for anyone, the plan was in place, everyone knew what was expected.

Jar, Saros, and Hemessean was to stand guard,

"Please look after yourself Rean, I love you so much." Said Hemessean, she kissed Rean on the neck bowed her head and let him go away towards the central part of the dark wood

"Stay safe Rean." Jar and Saros shouted

"Don't worry my friends, all will be well." Replied Rean and headed off into the darkness

Earlier Rean had talked to Saros telling him that if things went for the worst and he did not make it, that he should do his best to save his love Hemessean, Saros agreed.

Rean carried on into the woods, the stench was coming through Rean's mask, though he knew he had to carry on, the walk was becoming more difficult, the roots from the trees where so full of blood, so strong, they were choking the forest floor, Rean's boots where covered in blood, the stench was so over powering, though he carried on into the darkened hole.

Into the darkness he walks

So strong in mind sure never to fall

Mind and body so ready to fight

This evil shall not overcome his might

Standing within the blooded stench

Walking tall through misery and all

Eyes open ever so wide

Ready for anything that night

The only way was to enter the dark

That evil cutter was sure to be ready for a fight

Hungered for evil and pain he feeds

While Rean's power will overcome and stand

The next day

Rean stopped for a while and found his feet, he went into his pocket, and pulled out some notes he had wrote down, some of the words from the telepathists slabs that hung on the walls, some of the writings where talking about becoming the evil through the light, they Read,

One can find evil in many forms, though the worst kind of evil is the cutter stench, be careful never to fall to deep or you will never return to your loved ones.

Close your eyes and find your being, the self will fall from its safe home, this is the time to travel toward where thy needs, once you have found the host, stay strong and overcome the fight you feel, stand tall or you will never return. In the same way to abandon the host after your work is complete, find thy body quickly and see thy enemy fall.

Rean carried away into the darkness then suddenly standing not far from him was the cutter, the terrifying sounds from the poor tortured souls while the stench was over whelming, close and closer he walked until the cutter noticed Rean. The evil eyes moved strait towards Rean, there was no going back now, this was it, the cutter screamed out at Rean, the terrifying screaming echoing far into the wood, the darkness shivering with fear. Rean's hearts pounding with fear and excitement, he was about to battle with the purest of evil, the cutter started to move towards Rean, with a slow intimidating way to his walk, Rean close his eyes and became one with his shadow, and asked it to show his inner light strait to the cutter, Rean's light lifted from Rean's body, and his shadow kindly guided his light strait towards the cutter, Ream's light entered the cutter while the evil monster was screaming out his anger.

Now Rean was inside the deepest hole of evil, though he could not feel any pain, his inner self was too powerful, the light was making the cutter very angry, the stupid hulk of evil could not understand how or for that matter was happening, a battle within the mind, with the body, it was too much for the cutter.

Rean started to travel deep into the mind-set, and was replacing the dark matter into light matter, and once Rean had started it became easier, to guide the light matter, the cells where starting to overtake the darkness, the cutter had never know this, and was helpless, Rean's powers where so strong, while he planted the light within the dark, the cutter started to fall, the scream became less. Rean found the heart of the cutters evil, he knew this was the only way in and it would be difficult to get out once in, though he could not think of his self though for the people and friends around him.

Towards the evil black heart

Go deep within

Make true the light

And find thy fight

For the darkness will fall

And the light will win

The light shall win

The light shall win

Open everything new

Towards this path

Everything shall find it way

Show the dark its true light

Becoming all beautiful new

The new born light taking the dark away

When birth makes death cry

Forever light will shine

Sing thy song lighted one

Find the ever changing shifts of light

Within the beating hearts for love soaked shine

Find thy light darkness

Say goodbye darkened one

Now towards the new

Forever rising with the new

Oh beautiful everything within

Take away this shadowed one

And fill it light within

Within all new

186

I stand towards all

All of good

And ask for new

To find

And show this hulk of sickness

The love from within life

All true abandonment

Shall it be with you?

Find thy darkened heart and say goodbye

I plant thy light within you

Stand within you and feel thy grow

Feel thy grow

I am no monster within you

This is true with light

That grows and overcomes you

Feel this now

Feel thy heart of light all good

Know within you

187

Feel this wonder I plant inside

Towards the ever-changing

You become

You become

You become

Rean now had the cutter it was only a matter of time before Rean and the cutter was to join and become one, Rean had to escape now,

"I must find thy strength, and pull away, now, now, I must do it now!"

To the edge of darkness he pulls away

Clouded judgments

Feeling dizzy

"Must find myself"

Pull harder from this darkness

He must pull harder

Find a way to pull away from this evil, the light is becoming very strong he must find his way to overcome this and find the way out.

Towards the ever-changing

Pulling from the core of evil the heart, was difficult, though somehow Rean found strength and gave his light one more pull.

Shafts of energy flew from Rean hearted light finding all new becoming, this all new spark became so strong, with in the darkness was a shine like no other, the cutter fell like and old tree blown by the wind, the darkness could not take the light and power any more, drifting towards the gowned the cutter closed its eyes for the last time.

Rean had done it, overcoming the purest of evil the cutter was no more; Rean was finding his way out of the cutters being he was strong, stronger that he'd ever been the light was on Rean's side showing him the way, though Rean felt differently than before,

"I feel like I have been here before, but how could this be?" Rean ask himself

Somehow Rean was becoming within the light so much stronger that when he first entered the cutter, it was like the cutters powers fell away from the cutter and went into Rean, though only the light could answer this, as Rean was leaving the cutters being something new happened, Rean started to go into something new, it wasn't the same light as when he entered the cutter, this was more powerful, in its shine and glow finding Rean.

Rean was becoming something stronger than he ever thought. He was in fact finding the inner light, the path.

Chapter Ten

Rean finds his path

Towards something new, guided into the light, finding what he was, the way had always been set out for Rean, he just had to be pointed towards his destiny, after leaving the corpse of the cutter Rean's being had become the next part of his light, his path was closer, and all was well, now so strong nothing really could stop this light, the light was ever so bright.

This shine that finds you

With everything new

Inside your being

To serve the good

To find the dark

Never ending lighting all

Well to the sky

Find thy self within all

Now to this he goes

Within all bright standing true

Love and forever

This power of everything

Rean stand tall towards the path

Finding everything and all

Within this song

What could go wrong?

Now he was in deep towards the Path, a place of the pure, the light, and only a place where one was asked, no one could ever just go their they had to have extreme powers of high and extraordinary insight towards the path of light, only the true all powerful had requested Rean to find them.

Who was inviting Rean? And why did they want him to stay in the light, by now he should have returned to his physical being, though he was traveling deep within the light, feeling new and ever so strong, so many questions where fly inside Rean's inner mind, Rean just kept going deeper and deeper into the light, he couldn't see anything in front of him, he was just being pulled by something, so he carried on going, fling deeper and deeper into the all-powerful.

He could feel a new sensation touching him and was becoming knowing, something was trying to communicate with Rean, he knew that everything was for a good reason and nothing would hurt Rean, so with his all-powerful light just went with it and carried on, towards the middle of this new brightened shine was a voice, the sound was beautifully new sending away surprise in it song, a truly fantastic sound, beckoning Rean closer and closer, he went forwards towards this new light, this new sound a voice called   from   the   light,

"Rean we call for you, we need your help, where from far away, far from the earth where you live, where from a place that was long ago, when time was just starting we grew, we have been observing you for some time now, knowing that we would someday want your help, you now hold such a power and have proved you devotion to the all true light of living, we have come to find your being and in hope that you will help us, for years and years our world has been looking for light, the all-powerful light that will someday put a stop to all death and hate, and after seeing you over the past years and what you have achieved, we know that you can help our populaces grow into the true all being light and find true peace with life."

Rean knew that everything so far in his journey towards the path had sent him in good stead, and that to find the goodness from all being love, is the truth, so anyone asking for help to find their way into the all being truth of forever light should be helped and he cried out,

"to the light in your eyes and the new energy within my beating heart I send to my answered that is yes, oh, my most humble yes, for the light will shine into the forever, and we shall plant thy seed within the new born and show our true light towards the all being sun lighted sky, them if can be of use to you, I shall say yes, towards the new day of tomorrow you shall take me and let me do my work, let my arm hold out the light towards the forever love   within   your   hearts."

The sounds of beauty and rejoice, sounded out from the approaching lighted gaze,

"we shall come for you soon Rean, you will bring helpers, you will bring two of your close friends and on the second day after you go to them, we shall come for you, now go well Rean, we shall send you back to your physical body where you will find your own again, remember tell thy friends, and be ready on the second day, on the second day."

The voice faded, Rean began to fall downwards towards earth and back within his physical being, Rean opened his eyes, and looked around, he could see the corpse of the cutter, lifeless, so much anger and now nothing, Rean turned and walked away back towards his good friends, Jar, Saros, and Hemessean, they were faithfully waiting for him, Rean Ran to them and shouted,

"My good friends I thank you, from my heart, it is done, the cutter is no more, we have overcome this darkness, with our love, and within our true light we overcame the darkness."

Jar, Saros, and Hemessean, looked in amazement and of joy they shouted back,

"Rean, oh...Rean, we are so happy for today shall shine for many days to come, let it be known on this day light overcame the darkness and found true light, oh...Rean."

Rean found them jumping and dancing with each other, Rean looked in Hemessean's eye's and said,

"My love, today it feels so wonderful to look into your wonder again, my heart is complete with you I see everything new so richer, and my friends Jar and Saros, we now can go back to Casszoolas and tell them that all shall be well, let us, set away now, let us tell them the good news."

They set back meeting up with Warham and the lighted opals and travelled swiftly back to Casszoolas, with the great news many celebrations where to come, all night long. While everything was joyfully dancing with love, Ennin welcomed Rean and the others with open arms telling them that as soon as the cutter was killed all of the negative nasty's fell into the dusted ground and was never seen again, Ennin and the great council gave Rean and the others the key to Casszoolas, letting them and any of their loved one to stay and live within the way of Casszoolas at any time. The king gave Rean and the others his hand and his heart for all light in the everywhere and told Rean that peace would be the words from now on in the wall of Casszoolas.

Rean wanted to talk to his good friends Jar, Saros, and Hemessean, he asked them to meet him as soon as they could, there was no time he knew the others were coming for him the very next day, he knew that he could only take two of them and one would have to stay behind,

"My dear friends, I have asked much of you, and now I shall do so again, we are the protectors of the light and in doing so we hold much in our hearts, I have been ask by the far away people for help, they have been watching us for some time and spoke to me while I was within the light, not long ago, I was asked for help, and I accepted, I need two of you to come with me, we shall be taken tomorrow, who will come with me?." Rean asked

Hemessean, instantly walked forwards and said,

"I will follow you Rean, into the light, into everywhere, I shall give you my heart, my love, and my being is your being.

Saros and Jar both wanted to also come along side, though Rean knew that Saros has not long since married and also born a child with his wife, so Rean ask Saros to stay and look after his new family, Saros obeyed Rean's wishes to stay behind.

"My good friends it will soon be time to travel once again, so for now we should enjoy our time, go now and make joy, dance and bee free, fall into the nights dance, I will see you soon, and we shall find our next journey within this light." Said Rean

Hemessean took Rean's hand and led him away into the night where they enjoyed the night joys, with love and dance, their passions carried them into the early morning, making love till light, it was soon time to start the new day, they awoke, together lying naked after a night of passion, they both washed and enjoyed their breakfast, it was soon time to meet up with Jar, and get ready to start their next part of their journey, Rean was told to find a tree and old tree and they would be found, he was told,

"Find a tree, and we shall find you, we shall come for you

We shall come for you

They set away towards an old tree, one of the oldest trees Rean knew of in Casszoolas, Rean looked at the others and said,

"We must make a circle, join hands with me and make a circle around this old tree."

They all held hands and made it around the old tree with just enough space around the tree, they stud and waited, it wasn't long before they felt a reverberation coming from above, Rean looked up and said,

"There hear, it's time my friends, do not worry everything will be fine."

Rean's reassuring words where true they had nothing to worry about it was the far away people coming for them, they came from far, far away, deep from, darkest stars, the all-knowing wisdom from long ago, when earth was just in the making, the gasses forming and making new life, that is where the far away people come from.

Rean, Jar and Hemessean looked up and gazed at a large ship, coming towards them, in its appearance it could have been described at three orbs coming into each other, the ship was truly massive. Closer and closer the ship of the far away people came, until the ship was just above Rean, Jar and Hemessean sending a ray of light onto them, this was the transporting light, a light that could hold any kind of human form and send them into the ship, the transporting light found Rean, Jar and Hemessean and held them towards the ships opening, taking them deep within the ship, Rean, Jar and Hemessean where now in the ship of the far away people and ready to start there new journey deep into the stars to help with the fight and bring the protection where needed.

The ship of the far away people

They became aware that they had arrived deep into the centre of the ship, it was so enormous, Rean opened his eyes and was looking at the far away people, they just looked like humans, though they all looked the same? Rean asked,

"Why do you need us, for what way can we help you?"

A voice came from a speaker hanging above them and replied,

"Don't stress my friends, all will be seen soon please follow us into the guard room, where we shall meet you and tell you all, please follow us."

One of the far away people held his hand out and signed Rean, Jar and Hemessean to follow them into the guard room, so they followed them into a large room, where siting in a chair was a large man , he said,

"Welcome my friends, welcome to our ship we will be on our way soon, we have much to talk about and we thank you for coming with us, and for your help, my name is Emesis captain of the ship, please, at the moment you all need to go to a safe place in the ship, where you will all sit in safety so that we can travel through light and time, so please follow me."

Rean, Jar and Hemessean were escorted to pod like seats and were asked to sit in them while they travelled to Diahotus a world deep within the lighted stars, far from anything they had known before, it was so far from there world, the only way to the planet was through light travel, and that had to be done using speeds that only could be achieved with their high adapted technology for years and years of inventing and studying.

They were placed into their pods to sit and wait; it was soon time to go into the light towards Diahotus.

Time into light

Through the power of life

Spinning deep with the sight

All the far away technology

Taking them deeper and deeper

Faster and faster

Within all lighted shine

Knowing there in good hands

Flowing into the unknown

In their minds

What will be asked next?

With an excitement

Of the all-seeing new

These beauties shine and are true

After traveling deep within the lighted space they found their way into Diahotus, a truly beautiful world, this kingdom of light they had found, what wonder, what delight found them, the ship docking into an immense glass city scape, a true wonder to see, masses and masses of city scape's on top of each other a city of what looked like glass, though you could not see through it, protected from any disturbance, a true splendour of spectacular construction and development of truly amazing phenomenon of creativity and mammoth architectural splendour.

This vision was staggeringly impressive, they had found a phenomenal way to live, of many that only dream of back where Rean and the others lived,   Rean, Jar and Hemessean where overcome with the fantastic all around them, cities on metropolises, all living in the light, a true way of life, Rean and the others were taken to the quarters of 7 where they all sat and waited for someone to meet them.

After a short wait the door opened and a tall figure entered, it was Lettttt the one, he was the one to talked to Rean when he was in the light, inside the cutter,

"Welcome Rean and I see you have friends with you please stand one at a time and show yourself."

First Hemessean stud and greeted Lettttt,

"Good day I am Hemessean protector of the light." She said standing proudly

Next to stand was Jar,

"My name is Jar also protector of the light, it is wonderful to be invited into your world." Said Jar

Rean   stud   and   asked,

"We are all keen on why you have asked us hear, everything appears to be abundant with life and light, why have we been asked hear?"

"we have asked for your help because not everything is at first glance hear in Diahotus, many of our people have not been told about our troubles, we simply do not want them to worry so we have asked you to help us, we have been observing you for a while and looking at how you fight the darkness, your use of positive through the negative is very impressive you hold a true power, that many would love to have, and you use it to protect the light from all darkness, this has been why we have asked you for help, many because we feel that you can do what we ask, we have a growing darkness like a cancer with the beautiful planet, it is not far away from the negative nasty's, that once lived on your world, until you so greatly rid your world of them, our darkness is known as, *The Endings* a true form of evil, they feed on us like you do when hungry, please I warn you, many of my people have been taken by this evil, and never been seen again, this darkness, has been hidden from most of our people for the fear of panic sends shivers down my spine, we need to protect them." said Lettttt

"What do they look like, and where would we find them?" asked Rean

Lettttt showed Hemessean, Jar and Rean a drawing of the evil Ending,

"Why, they look like this."

The Endings

Rean and the others looked at the hideous darkness that was known as the endings, they had not seen evil like this before.

"The endings, they dwell deep within the shadows of our world, not many see them until it is too late, like the negative nasty, they find there victim and urge on their goodness, the poor unknowing falls quickly to the three ways and is taken before they can do anything about it, this is true evil so please be careful." Said Lettttt

"Can someone take us to where they dwell?" ask Rean

"Yes, Rean, not just now, first we need to take you to see, one that we have taken prisoner, it is under spell of light so it cannot attack anyone, come with me." Replied Lettttt

Rean, Jar and Hemessean set away following Lettttt and the guards deep with the underground of Diahotus, where only evil could be kept; it was truly a dark place.

They walked for a long while until they found the dark prison; they were met by a strange sounding hale, echoing around the walls, Lettttt shouted,

"Open!"

And with that the cell doors started to open, very slowly as the doors where very heavy so nothing could get out, this was truly a prison for the darkest of evil ever seen, it was hell under guard, nothing was going to get out of this old cell. The door opened and inside was standing in some kind of slow motion unconsciousness was the ending, it was drifting in and out of sight, like a light bulb that was just about to die, and the ending was the same, this evil was starved of the dark just like the negative nasty, though the endings where much more advanced in there ways of evil.

"This   is   a   Ending,"   said   Lettttt

Rean walked close to the cell window and spoke to the ending,

"Tell me ending, what do you want from the people of Diahotus? Why do you bother them so?"

Shivers found the sell, this evil was about to talk to Rean,

"You...you, I know of you...you, I want your light...Your light will be my darkness."

Shouted the ending

"Shock it, quick weaken it!" shouted Lettttt

One of the guards gave the ending a quick shock of light; this made the ending sick with nothing and was soon ready to answer Rean.

Rean shouted,

"Tell me ending, why do you bother my new friends of Diahotus?"

The ending was in no state to not answer Rean; he let out a whimper, and then said,

"we want to overtake all, the light sickens us, you and all your kind, sicken us, your stench should never walk within the light, you all should be beaten until you're ready for the dark then we should take you all away to die...die, die!"

"I knew I could never get a true intelligent answer from such filth as your kind, tell me why...tell me now!" shouted Rean

He punched the walls with both hands with anger at the ending.

"We...want your path...we shall have your light...you, will never win...I shall...die, now!"

And with that the ending burst in flames, laughing and screaming, until there was just a small heap of dust in the middle of the cell, a darkness found Rean, and he thought to himself,

"Why would it want to put itself through that much pain? Why? I don't understand everything."

Rean was clearly shocked and asked if he could be taken somewhere where he could be alone and meditate for a while, he needed to find himself again and find reason for this question, and he knew that doing this would help him find an answer that would help in the plan to defeat the ending.

Rean was taken away to a chamber, where he could find new energy and meditate; he was placed within the straightforwardness chamber where Rean sat in the middle and started to open up his being,

Let in thy light

Show me

Show my self

All and around

Free me and find me

Open in energy new

Light of everything

All into one

We shall find true light

Within this is everything

I see this

And feel within

All new

Surrounded by everything within

This sound of all anticipating touch

Through this thinking I see new

See what I wanted to

Show me

Stay thy shine

And feel all around

Emending the darkness

True heart in mind

Finding all light sky

This dance from all over

Finds everyone

Towards beating true

From distance to new

We hold everything with

Set it free

Set it free

Sound thy love, thy heart beat

Rean found his inner self, and was asking many questions, he knew that to defeat the endings he would need all power from light and above, for this he would have to be totally in control of his physical being as well as his total organism structured making, Rean knew that he would need to find, the energy of the endings and become that energy, like he did the cutter, that was the only way to destroy such an evil entity.

"I must find true peace in mind, all flowing design with in my own physical map, I feel strong though feel something is missing from my energy and should look deeper within the body, to find the   all   true   light   within."

In the sanctum of his mind Rean found his path towards light, the personification from his making, all abandonment should be found, this very reason for life and all light sounds from within can only be, with truth from everywhere, a sounding from the never ever would be a weakness within his plan, only the way into the true ways of light for fullness could be flourished and achieved through the positive thinking, from all and everywhere this can be found, and from that Rean found new Energies dancing within the lighted day that surrounded him within his ambient sincerity, that for what you must know, the way within darkness to pull away and make light in hole, then finding truth from negative is where we find all answering questions, this guardian from light and time is within him around his everywhere, the importance is an significance within meaning and all wellbeing, the profound knowledge of light into all truth is within the distance that is whitened abandonment.

Rean looked deep within himself and walked towards his path, finding within all truth and asked,

"Within me, thy light I ask you this, why is it I feel I need more from the path? I stand on this day with all my heart and say to you, hold me true my friend within, you have done well, know all and everything good that has been before, oh...guided one, show me where I can find the part of what is missing from my heart?" asked Rean to self

"all true abandonment can be found as complete forgiving and rewarding energy new, we hold so many strengths with us, I stand within you all the time, no this path, this stronghold within, come to own, find this lighted sole, look deep from within, and see everything true." Called from within

The light-minded can show us many doorways and through dream, day of night will hold secrets within its concert, this is known as the dream weaving, a fundamental importance of the knowing, your path is always ready to find you, though only through vision and dream can we achieve answers, because when dream is happening, we unlock all our obstructions when awake in the living world, seal thy work of all being from dream and show self the doorway, and walk through this way, the answer is waiting for you, in meditation all energy's find the truth from mind body and soul, a combination from the living to the path, walk and find your answer.

Rean closed his eyes and soon became within, all lighted sounds found him drifting next to his being, a wonderful dance, and formations into all seeing being the calculations of in the making that started life, all energy's found Rean this started a new dance within his beating heart, sending new vibrant vibrating electric pulses into his brain waves, sending new effervescent thoughts into his being.

Rean felt so new his path was true and gave him the new energy that he wanted, feeling like himself again, the light that he felt had disserted him was now back with him, dancing around his mind, a complete wonder that found him within meditation.

New effervescent thoughts found Rean

Deep within the mind can hold many doors, some open when using the all-seeing light, when the doors open, you don't have long before they shut, so to make the best from the opening you have to travel through as soon as you can.

Rean had been within his mind for some time and found the experience very useful, it was time to meet up with the others and strike up a plan.

Hemessean was waiting outside for Rean,

"Hello Rean, did you find everything you were looking for?" asked   Hemessea

"Yes, it was most enlightening; I travelled deep into my mind and found many answers"

"What should we do next?" Asked Hemessean

"We need to go find the others, I have a plan to find the endings and we need to get to it straight away." Said Rean

"I have missed you Rean, it has been a few days since we talked, held each other, and it is crazy how I miss you when you're not with me." Said Hemessean gazing into Rean's eyes

"Yes Hemessean, I have true deep feelings for you too, though we have to be strong in hard times, we must not just think of our own feelings, and concentrate on the together things going on at the moment." Replied Rean with a faithful look in his eyes

"Please, forgive me Rean, I have been egotistical and full of my own feelings, oh Rean it is so easy to forget what danger we are all in, love can blur many things out, I know I have to be stronger." Replied Hemessean

"My beautiful friend, we will have many days of love to come, all we need to do is stay focused on what is asked of us and after we have finished what has been ask of us then it will be time for our love to show its way." Said Rean kissing Hemessean's neck

"Rean you are quite wonderful, I feel stronger just been next to you, yes…we shall stay focused, and I shall try to stop my feelings over taking my mind, I understand now that our mission to stop this evil is what we should be thinking about." Replied Hemessean kissing Rean back on his lips and holding Rean close

"My dear Hemessean… I want you right now though we have to be strong and hold this passion…oh Hemessean I want you so bad." Rean pushed himself closer to Hemessean

"Oh, Rean…kiss me, hold me, and kiss me." Whispered Hemessean

Rean and Hemessean was both sexually aroused heavily kissing and touching each other, running through Rean's mind was that this could not happen, he had little time, his love and passion for Hemessean, and he was going to have to be strong and pull away from this wonderful embrace,

"Oh, Hemessean…we have to stop, oh…my love please we have to go now! Later we shall…later." Whispered Rean in Hemessean's Ear while stroking her hair

Hemessean looked into Rean's eyes and said,

"Yes, come let us go to the others and we can do this later," Hemessean was the first to pull away, and straiten her top

They found their composure and set away back to see if they could find Jar, and talk about the big plan.

Rean and Hemessean found their way back to the ship in the central part of Diahotus where Jar was waiting for them, Jar introduced Rean and Hemessean to Nathan elder of the Daham tribe, many years had Nathan been a tribe leader, he had seen many things in his serving, many battles, the true protector of Diahotus.

"Welcome back Rean and Hemessean, I trust you found what was wanted of you?" asked Jar

"Yes my friend and it is good to see you, and welcome Nathan, so you're the elder of the Daham tribe, we hope to be of use to your people, we have no time let us rest and talk about the plan against the endings." Replied Rean

Rean, Jar, Hemessean and Nathan, sat around the great table of Diahotus with Emesis and talked about how they would find strength in the fight of the endings.

"I need Nathan and Emesis army's to stand strong together, at the front in case of the endings having any of their negative nasty's as back up...we don't know how many they have, so we need to be ready, I know they will have everything we fear and we will have to be strong, for this day ahead of you will be testing for us all, me Hemessean, and Jar will go into the central part of the darkness, then I will have to go deep within the dark myself."   Said   Rean

"We must be strong, and follow Rean… Rean you can count on our army's till the last man or women, we will fight until our last breath." Said Nathan with pride in his voice

"My good people, so today we stand against evil like before, though this evil is so very dark, the last evil was so very difficult to defeat, though I have faith within my heart and I have faith within my friends, so I look upon you all today and say, stay strong…thing of the positive, and when darkness comes to find our hearts stay strong and show it the light, do not worry look it into the eye of darkness and show it strength within, I understand that some of us here today will fall into the darkness, and it is a heavy price to pay, though we have no other way to choose, I hold my heart and wish you all well, let us stand together and be as one of today is the day that we put away the evil ending…stay strong." Said Rean

"We shall go straight away to the front!" said Nathan

They all stud and walked out leaving Rean, Jar and Hemessean, Rean looked at his faithful friends and said,

"So here we are again…at the front of our day becoming ready for a new fight against the endings, I understand, that we have become so close, and Hemessean, we have almost become one within our love, though I have to ask you…please forget our love for today and become the guardian of the light that first met me all them nights ago, we have to be at our strongest and forget our love until we defeat the evil endings, and my good friend Jar, I also hold you in my heart...we have travelled many a way together, let us come together and go to the darkness, come my friends." Said Rean

They set away deep within the mountains of Diahotus, they knew the dark one was waiting, growing, his army or the sickened where feeding on the negatives flying around the depths of diseased minds, moulding into one massive abandonment of all hideous malevolent thoughts, Jar and Hemessean would have a fight on their hands holding the middle dominion, where many of the endings would be waiting, Rean would have to travel deeper with the darkness following the stench of darkness. Rean and the others had accepted in their minds that some of them would never see each other again, though to save so many it would have to be this way and nothing could be done otherwise, they travelled deeper into the darkness towards the layer of the endings.

Towards the end for some, and the fight had just begun, this scornful mess of darkened scream, twisting everything towards the never ever, the stench was becoming so bad

The endings

They had to put on their suits again; they could tell that it was soon, the fight of light was soon upon them.

The   utterings   of   the   endings,

"This stench of human flesh, this pain that walks in my heart, when we find you well be looking to serve you pain...pain that you have never felt before, human go for my home of darkness, stay away...humans I tell you once, then if you do not heed my warnings then hell will find you...hell will come for your heart and rip it out of that stink...out of you stench, humans I smell you...we shall find you, and end you!"

The chilling words from the endings where traveling through the darkness where Rean and the others were traveling, though they carried on with hope in their hearts, brave things.

"I don't doubt for one minute, the utterings coming from this darkness are true negative words, though our words will carry the light."

Rean held out his hands and projected new words into the darkness to combat the negative,

"Towards all beauty, we hold you, this darkness shall not find us, nor hurt thy friends, my petals come from the lighted houses of everything new, let them find this gloominess and send it on its way, towards the light, we shall follow you darkness, and we shall end you...towards the light for you, and all of your kind, so take your warning back and surrender your evil ways into the all new energies of everything new, look in front of you, look behind you...where coming for you, show thy self."

Rean and the others carried on into the darkness, this rotten part from everything decomposing of every step into the darkness, they had to be strong now and pull everything they knew together.

"Hemessean and Jar it is time for me to let you go, I have to go ahead by myself now, so please stay here and remember this, whatever happens, we have to do this and never fall or run from the darkness, always show the darkness the light, always!" said Rean

"Rean, we will do as you say, and stay here and wait for you, if we see any of the endings we shall show them our light...go well my friend." Said Jar

"Thank you my good friend...thank you!" replied Rean with a tear in his eye

"Oh, Rean...my love, please stay well...please take care, I will be lost without you...go with my love in your heart!" said Hemessean in tears

"My beautiful love Hemessean, do not cry, soon tomorrow will come with the new days light and in that light I shall be waiting for you, do not cry...stay strong within your mind, and help see away this darkness...do not let your love weaken your fight, stay strong my love." Said Rean, disappearing into the darkness

Hemessean shouts out,

"I   will   Rean,   I   will!"

And with that Rean went into the darkness, Hemessean and Jar prepared for any arrival of any kind of the darkness.

Jar looked at Hemessean and said,

"let us show this evil our way of the true light, let us not shed any more tears and show that we are strong and well, Hemessean stand with me and send out the everything light."

Hemessean and Jar stud together and held out there hands, spraying out there everything light through the darkness; they would be safe…for now.

Rean was on his own again, he knew the darkness was getting closer, the negative mutterings where getting stronger and stronger,

"Come then, Rean, come to us, Rean…Rean, we are waiting for you, come to us."

This was not effecting Rean's concentration; he was reciting words from one of the all-knowing books from the time library, a volume of the writings of the great writer J.M.D she was well known for her chanting's of light ways, the light ways could cut through any kind of virus of negative uttering, he was repeating them over and over,

Towards the dark I send

Towards the dark we dance

This light will end you

This light will cure them…

Towards the dark I send

Towards the dark we dance

This light will end you

This light will cure them…

Towards the dark I send

Towards the dark we dance

This light will end you

This light will cure them…

Rean was not worried; he knew that everything in the past was helping him through this darkness and that he was strong, ever so strong, every time Rean had defeated fragments of the darkness he grew stronger, turning the darkness into light. Every day the growing of his light had become more profound than ever.

"This light in my home, this stench how dare you come to my home, you bastard child...I see that you hold love in your miserable heart, you bastard...I will take your love from you and kill...

Kill,

kill... you make me sick, your light, what a bastard you are, when I take your lover I shall cut her into two and watch her life fall away, then I shall plague her flesh and suck the pungent mess into this darkness forever...forever, do you hear me Rean?...Forever!"

"Hemessean is safe; she is ok" Rean said to himself

Then Rean shouted at the ending,

"Cowered, show yourself...show yourself, you talk of evil though we both know that light will overcome your evil ways every time, wear are you ending, where do you hide?"

"Rean,

Rean,

Where   right   next   to   you."

Rean didn't have his protective forever lighting on, he wasn't ready for this, and the ending had Rean thinking too much about his love, Hemessean, something touched Rean's arm, something had injected something in his upper limb,

The pain was excruciating sending shocks through Rean's body sending him slumping to the ground,

Fighting for breath, Rean had been injected by the ending with its tail end,

"I...must...

       Find

        Strength"

Rean was fighting for his life, normally the poison from the endings tail would have killed anyone else, though Rean was in a lot of pain, though very strong, he soon found his feet and shouted out,

"It   will   take   more   than   that!"

And quickly adorned hid everything light,

"Know me darkness, know my name, come back and I shall show you the light, know my name."

The twisting and turning of darkness pain find all around within all the insane,

Playing with your feeling,

And taking your love,

Sending far away from all and above,

Only the strong will find their way,

Put away this dark cloud and follow the light always ready to win your fight,

The ending is everywhere we go,

Playing with the thoughtful into yesterday and showing it today,

Don't let it do this, take control of your own way,

Through this life time we stand,

In speeding hand in hand,

No one will stop to help for too long,

It's truly up to you to find your way,

And show the negatives on their way.

Remember the words from this tale,

In story we must carry on and help the other make right where darkness is doing wrong.

Rean jumped into the loud foreboding darkness knowing what was behind its mask,

"Show yourself."

Rean suddenly found himself standing in the hive of the endings, a mass of hovering creatures, flew above Rean's Head, with a human torso and a the rest of its structure was a body of some strange kind of insect, a truly hideous creature of the darkest hive from evils heart, the fight was about to begin for the light and good of all living kind, Rean was standing in the heart of evil where he knew that the everything could go wrong if he wasn't strong, so Rean looked deep within his heart and found his everything, he remembered everything he was given, from the grounding in negative into positive.

The way into the light was his method of fight, no gun or man-made weapons would be of help to Rean in this fight, he needed the power of *mind and being*.

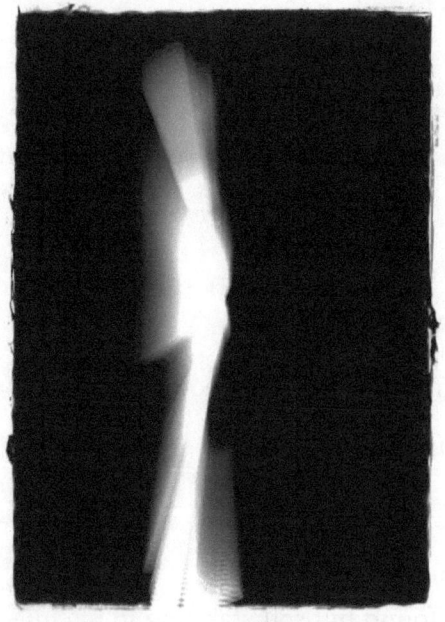

Mind and being

Meanwhile Emesis and Nathan and the tribe of Daham go deep within the mountains of Diahotus to fight the army of the lost souls.

Nathan Tribe Elder

Towards the opening they walk, with all of the tribes of Diahotus ready to fight for everything they believe in, and the fight ahead will be a brutal battle going head to head with the evil army of the lost souls, an army of evil fighters with nothing to lose and nothing to gain, the lost souls are under the spell of the endings, all they know is to fight and destroy everything in their way, and they are ready and hungry to do so. Nathan and Emesis and the tribes wait for the cry to attack and within seconds the cry is sounded,

"For Diahotus, for the light!" shouted Nathan

The cries of war echoed down the mountains it had begun, the battle for light and love were now woken, both armies of many different tribes in a row after row, ran towards the sickened army of the lost souls. Within seconds they met with anger...with pride the Daham tribes where brutal in there attack nothing could be done, it was war and this evil had to be stopped, the battle went on...

While the battle carried on in the side of mountains of Diahotus Jar and Hemessean where prepared for their fight with more of the evil endings sent to get them, Jar and Hemessean where ready for a fight, completely aware of what was coming through the darkness...this evil mass, the stench of everything bad was coming for them, nothing could be done to stop the fight, they knew it would be vicious and cruel, the endings are made for one

231

thing and that is war and pain, to commit pain and suffering to whom ever got in there way, the endings where ordered to fight to the death, and they were coming with the hunger of death in there dark hearts, it was not long before Jar and Hemessean could feel the presence of evil,

"Jar...listen, can you hear that?" said Hemessean

"Yes, it's them, get ready Hemessean, and remember use the light within...the light within!" shouted Jar

A haunting sound found them...a voice, intimidating in its character,

"Be still; do not move, where here to kill, killing is what we love, I can smell two, one for me and one for you...stand still and be slayed" echoed out from the darkness

"Oh, light make me strong, hold me through this fight, and show me the darkness so I can fight." Said Hemessean

From the darkness came out four endings swarming around Jar and Hemessean, both protected with their everything light, Jar looked directly at one of the endings and said,

"Darkened one so you have come, let me send you away far into deaths might, where all you will find is the nothing, your ending is   tonight."

With that Jar sent his everything light deep into the unprotected endings darkened heart, with and instant the ending fell in agony and screamed out in pain and shattered into ashes.

"You bastard of the light, we shall now come for you." Said the endings

Behind Jar and Hemessean where a new swarm of endings and quick to the touch they let out a spiral of dark energy's, so strong so evil, in its method, luckily Jar and Hemessean where ready for anything and combated it with more light surrounding them, though they did not expect the ending to also come from the darkness stench of the ground, Jar fell instantly,

"They have me Hemessean; I cannot do anything I have been stung by one of them, Hemessean, help me…help me."

Hemessean quickly found Jar, she was trying to help him though it was too difficult, Jar was going to die in seconds, her friend that she had been with for so long was going to die, right in front of her and Hemessean had many of the ending surrounding her, though inside of Hemessean was strength and determination,

"You evil scum…you won't take me like that." shouted out Hemessean

Sadly Jar faded and died next to Hemessean's feet as she carried on fighting the endings, she didn't have time to say goodbye to Jar, Hemessean was fighting for her life also, everywhere where the evil endings all around her, just as Hemessean thought it was the end… a new light found her, it was the telepathist's come to save her, the ending where no match, against Hemessean and the telepathist's, they soon had a controlled fight on their hands,

"Thank you my friends, Rean had talked to me about you… I thank you; I thought I was done for…thank you."

Hemessean had time to find her dead friend Jar,

"Oh…Jar, I will miss you, so very much, with my heart I tell you we shall win this fight, go find your friend Frestro tell him how you fought the darkness for the light."

A rest period found Hemessean, she went to the telepathist's, they had seen away the endings, for now they had time to rest before they came back with more fight in there evil hearts. They found a peaceful area and laid to rest Jar, now it was just telepathists and Hemessean, she wondered if Rean was ok,

"Oh…Rean, stay strong, Jar is with Frestro now…stay strong my love."

Hemessean looked down at Jars grave and said,

I stand here

With you

Oh my friend

Already I miss you

You have not died in vain

We shall overcome this darkness

And see the true light

This night is so full of dread

As we lay your head

My friend

Rest know

Sleep for a while

Before you're away

To live again

In another

Sleep now

Lay my friend

This darkness will not last

Light is with us

In death

In life

Seek the light and find life

235

Rest my friend

Hemessean walked slowly away and bowed her head. The telepathists comforted her and said,

"Stay strong Hemessean, we shall win this fight, do not lose heart, and rest for we will soon have a new fight on our hands, stay strong and rest."

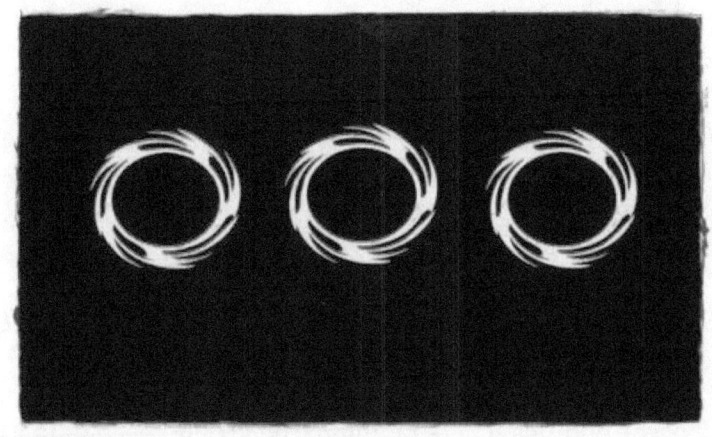

The Telepathists

Hemessean closed her eyes and fell deep asleep, while closely watched over by the telepathists.

Meanwhile

Rean had his own fight on his hands, the endings where strong, every thoughtless evil hearted belongings they fronted Rean telling him that they had just killed his good Friend Jar. Such an evil thing to do, now it was playing with his mind, though Rean also knew that that is what the endings wanted him to do, so Rean put everything away for now, knowing that Jar would not want Rean to die in the same way as he was. Rean found his strength within himself and stud strong against the endings,

"I see you evil, I hear you evil, and I smell you evil, Hear me evil when I say to you...you will be gone, and sooner than you think."

Rean shone his light strait into the chest of one of the larger endings; this sent the ending crashing into the darkened ground exploding into ashes, and did the same too many more of the endings, it was Rean using his power of the negative into positive, and it soon became apparent who was going to overcome the other.

Many of the endings where falling to the ground becoming ashes, embers of the darkness, fallen to the path. The night was growing colder by the minute, the stench of death was everywhere, the hopelessness of sadness trying to attack Rean's mind, though he was too strong for any such thing, he was ready for more, nothing was going to stop him now, more and more of the endings where falling, Rean wanted to find the Queen ending, if he could destroy this evil one, then he knew the rest would fall, though he carried on with the killing, it was an intense fight, many had fallen from Rean's light though many where still attacking him, over and over they came from all directions, it was a true fight, Rean was using everything he had inside of his being, so determined that he would win this fight, and nothing would stop him, a true fight between the dark and the light, many had already fallen, and Rean was still in good strength for more of the same.

"Come on...show yourselves evil, I want more, come on, come see my light, hear me...you will all soon fall by my might! Feel my light, show yourselves evil, and let me end you!"

From all directions the ending attacked, it looked never-ending and they came with true hatred within their hearts, this battle for the power of all life was at its worst, death and suffering everywhere, Rean just stepped up and went forwarded deeper and deeper into the fight, into the darkness knowing soon he would come across the queen of the endings and put a stop to this madness.

What would become of everyone if Rean and the other failed, there was no option but to go deeper and deeper into the fight, this pain, this never-ending battle, Rean battled through the endings leaving piles of ashes where they had fallen, the smell of death was everywhere, with this he knew that he was starting to get somewhere, shorty he would find the queen, this tangled mess of evil stench, would soon be confronted with the purest of light, it would blind her, leaving the queen with nothing but death. Rean knew that to find the queen would be no easy task, she would no doubt be guarded by many of the endings and they wouldn't let him any were near the queen, still the ending kept leaping out at Rean, there was so many of them, each one so strong and so determined in killing Rean.

"I have to be strong and work my way through this, I know deep down in my heart everything will work out for the light deep within my heart and that the sound of love will ring out towards our sun blessed sky's once again, destroying all of this darkness, all of this negative shall be gone and for good."

Think positive thoughts Rean went deeper within the darkness.

Meanwhile

Deep within the mountains the Battle against the army of the dead souls went on with many falling from both sides, it was a truly horrific battle. Emesis had being killed within the fight with many of his comrades, Nathan was still deep within the battle line with his tribe fighting with a passion, with a passion that they would overcome the darkness and that the light, the all true light would overcome this darkness, they carried into the fight with beating hearts a strong and with love for everything good.

Towards and inwards, the fight for the survival of the light would go on for many days all three battles as difficult as the next, though even that they had suffered great loss, of friends and life, they went on deep into the darkness, fighting for everything they believed in so that one day the light would shine again and carry everything new towards the next day, and that there children could live on and be content without the threat of evil looming   above   them.

The three battles had been going on relentless for over a day, still the evil attacked, Rean was going deeper into the darkness in hope to find the queen of the endings, while Hemessean was still fighting some of the other endings, and Nathan battled through the Arms of the lost souls.

It was truly hell on the mountains, with many falling and never to stand again.

Towards the dark they fight

Never stopping within this unforgiving hell

Evil was after the light

Hold true Rean and the others

A fight within all

This burning hell

Time running by

Towards the never ending burn

Face deep in dead friends

The screams from lost souls

Run

Run away

They scream

240

Run, run away

We want your heads

The scream out

Though they know

The light will never

Give in

It's a fight within

Towards all-knowing light

This shall be done

Soon and forever new

Wanting the new light to

Shine through

This beautiful new

Will grow once again

Like the before

Holding its new born forever and a day

Hemessean and the telepathists, where hard at the fight, many of the endings had fallen in the misty knighted dust, though as quick as the evil ending appeared again and again Hemessean was becoming very tired, though she would not let the endings see that she was weakening.

"You're not going to win, it's just a matter of time before we win, give up and die, we want to end you!" shouted one of the endings

"Never, if you look at yourselves and see what is coming out of the darkness, then you will see the true nothing within you, why you're all really nothing aren't you, look at yourself…nothing!" shouted Hemessean

"Nothing, was it nothing that ended your friends life? Yes we must be something don't you think? Replied the ending

"Evil, sick…yes though really your all just bad energy, completely waste of everything, give up now, know your end!" shouted Hemessean

With that Hemessean sent out a gigantic burst of light from the deepest part of her heart, it was from the goodness that had made her being, she knew that this would put a stop to what was ever talking to her, and Hemessean was right, the light had taken out many of the endings, leaving a path of black ash, cracking a hole deep within the endings defences, Hemessean could see for miles, her wonderful light was shining the darkness away,

"So you see you're nothing! Just ash…" Hemessean shouted out

The army of the lost souls where struggling to keep up with Nathan and his tribe, they were so very strong in the fight of light, the army of the lost souls could not understand why they were losing the fight, never before had anyone overcome their army. Something was weakening them and helping Nathan and his tribe.

That something was Rean, he was not only helping Nathan and the Tribe, but also his positive energies find his true love Hemessean, at last everything was going their way, Rean had sent out positive light energy's towards his friends without them knowing, he knew that after a while the defeat of each ending would strengthen Rean, and after a while he could send new energies out to his friends. This is called the positive reflex; the positive reflex could only be used by the all-knowing and seeing. Rean's new energies where becoming more intense as he slain the evil endings, anything in Rean's way would not stand a chance, this wonder of the fantastic, this light could never be stopped, Rean was not just human, he was the all energy authority and the growth within his heart was becoming stronger, more and more Rean would slay the evil in his way, the endings falling like fly's, though still they came attacking Rean, the stupidity of the endings was unmistakeable, the quicker Rean slayed them the more they came at Rean. The darkness was also very strong, more so for Rean, as he was getting closer to the queen and her Army where protecting her with everything they had, the endings just couldn't keep up even though they were very strong, Rean was too strong for them, he knew that he was getting closer

243

to the queen, and it was just a matter of time before he reach the queen of the endings.

"I will find the Queen and end her, end this darkness forever; this will be the last of the endings, the very end"

Rean had found his way to the centre of the hive, and he could see the Queen, surrounded by her army of endings, the dark energies where enormous, though Rean still carried on fighting into the very centre until it was just him and the queen, Rean stud up to the queen and said,

"Know me queen, I offer you the way of the light, I offer you peace from my heart, what do you say queen?"

The queen looked up and down at Rean and shouted,

"You offer nothing, human scum; you're not going to turn my dark heart into the stench of your ways! I will rip you apart, and then feed you to my army…human scum!"

The queen spat at Rean, and then closed her eyes conjuring a spell of darkness against him, though it did not do any good for her, as Rean was too powerful for her…and she knew it.

"once again I say queen, I show you my heart, take the light and stop the fight between, me and my friends, we have seen too much death today, let us bring peace on this day, let it stop now, what do you say queen, call away your troops and I shall go and let you go…what do you say queen?" asked Rean

Rean knew that he was too strong for the queen, and if she did not surrender he had no choice but to end her, he waited for her reply.

"No! I shall never give in, never…" shouted the queen and sent out a vile strip of venom towards Rean, completely missing him in her fit of rage, Rean did not want to kill her but he had to, to save the others, if the queen would not stop her army's then the only other way was her death and the queens death would put stop to the others.

Rean closed his eyes and said,

Towards this evil

I send my light

Towards this fight

End this evil

End it now

The light found the queen and she burst in flames, the light was too strong for her and she fell to the ground turning into ashes, after that her army's fell, the army of the lost souls didn't have any reason to fight as the queens spell had gone with her death so they just evaporated into the darkness, and so did the rest of the endings, Rean knew for now the darkness was over and he had completed what was asked of him. So he made his way back to Hemessean, eventually he found Hemessean and he thanked the telepathists for their help and paid his respects to his good friend Jar.

They made their way back to Diahotus, were Nathan and the surviving tribe where waiting, everything was good again, the darkness of Diahotus had gone with the death of the queen.

The grave of the endings

The endings, everything was good. The people of Diahotus showed Rean and the other much love, and laid out an impressive banquet, with much to eat and drink. Rean was tired and so was his love Hemessean,

"Oh Rean, I am so glad that your still with me on this night, the night that Jar will never see." Said Hemessean with tears in her eyes

"Yes my love, we shall miss him, come hear my love…" Rean held out his hands

Hemessean ran into Rean's arms and they hugged and kissed for a short while, they were both clearly warn out after all the fighting so they laid together and fell asleep to the sound of the celebrations of the people of Diahotus. As they slept, beside them a small standing bedside clock stands next to their dreams, inside the small clock with mischief afoot,

Tick, tick, tick…

Towards The Path

By Patrick O'Malley Burke

www.ingramcontent.com/pod-product-compliance
Lightning Source LLC
Chambersburg PA
CBHW020727210626
46807CB00016B/372